"I am saving u  own."

"You can save faster if you take me up on my offer to come work at the clinic," Dan reminded her.

She'd been considering it—and leaning toward saying yes.

The fact that working with the handsome, sexy doctor—who appeared to be unaware of just what kind of signals he was setting off—was a good opportunity for other reasons was something she chose not to explore at the moment.

Placing her hand in his, she said, "Okay, Doc, you've got yourself a deal."

She intended for it to be nothing more than two people shaking hands. Instead, she had the feeling she was opening the floodgates for something else.

She pulled her hand away as if she'd touched fire.

Because maybe she had.

Dear Reader,

Welcome back to Forever. It's time for Tina's story. You didn't think I'd forget her, did you? Tina was the reason her sister even discovered the town—and what her heart was missing. When we first met Tina she was a very confused single mother whose baby's father had just tried to kill both of them. The Tina who eventually emerged from that emotional train wreck became a stronger, more centered person, focused on her son rather than herself and her admittedly horrendous choice of a male companion. As we get back to her now, she is busy building up her life, getting an accounting degree and making plans for herself and her son. But the best-laid plans of mice, men and heroines are often led astray and the very handsome bump in Tina's road is Dr. Dan Davenport, a man who comes with his own secret baggage to become Forever's first doctor in thirty years. Is he just an obstacle, or something more? Come read and find out.

As ever, I thank you for reading (where would I be without you?) and from the bottom of my heart, I wish you someone to love who loves you back.

Best,

Marie Ferrarella

Recycling programs
for this product may
not exist in your area.

ISBN-13: 978-0-373-75350-5

THE DOCTOR'S FOREVER FAMILY

The Doctor's Forever Family

Marie Ferrarella

TORONTO NEW YORK LONDON
AMSTERDAM PARIS SYDNEY HAMBURG
STOCKHOLM ATHENS TOKYO MILAN MADRID
PRAGUE WARSAW BUDAPEST AUCKLAND

ABOUT THE AUTHOR

USA TODAY bestselling and RITA® Award-winning author Marie Ferrarella has written more than two hundred books for Silhouette and Harlequin Books, some under the name of Marie Nicole. Her romances are beloved by fans worldwide. Visit her website at www.marieferrarella.com.

Books by Marie Ferrarella

@Forever, Texas
*Cavanaugh Justice
**The Doctors Pulaski
‡‡Kate's Boys
§The Fortunes of Texas: Return to Red Rock
αThe Baby Chase
ααMatchmaking Mamas

To Patience and Sam.
May you have a lifetime plus
a day of happiness.

Chapter One

So this is Forever.

The thought echoed like a not altogether quiet mantra in Dr. Daniel Davenport's head. He stood on a ridge, staring down at the South Texas town with the somewhat ironically prophetic name of Forever.

Forever.

It sounded like a prison sentence.

Dan had pulled his newly purchased navy blue Mercedes sedan—a car he now realized was woefully out of step with the surrounding terrain—over to the side of the road for one last moment by himself. A last moment in which he still hadn't put on the mantle of commitment, making himself one with the town that eagerly awaited his arrival.

Well, technically, they weren't awaiting *his* arrival, he thought wryly. They were waiting for Warren's. But that wasn't about to happen. He would have given his own life to make Warren appear, but the man was now in a place where his presence could not be won by bartering and promising everlasting servitude. He knew that for a fact because he'd tried. Tried praying and pleading, promising to do whatever was needed of him if only Warren could be spared.

But Warren was gone.

Gone because, at the last moment, he'd managed to prevail upon his younger brother, managed to physically drag him away from packing up all his belongings in preparation for his journey to Forever. Instead, he'd gotten Warren to agree to go out for a night of celebration.

After all, they had both just finally graduated. Graduated *everything:* medical school, internships, residencies. Everything. They had done it, taken all the necessary steps that finally, finally brought them to this new threshold shimmering before them. They had jumped all the hurdles, completed all the tasks and marched proudly into the winners' circle where they were both decorated with the well-earned and still, even in this day and age, enviable title of *Doctor.*

He and Warren had made the journey together despite the fact that he, Daniel, was a year older. It had taken him a year to figure out what he wanted to do with himself after he'd graduated from college, so he'd started medical school late, making it into those rarified waters by the skin of his teeth.

Dan sighed, shaking his head. It was all a blur now, but he'd been a carefree devil in that last lifetime. Brilliant but frivolous. So much so that of all the schools he'd applied to, he'd only gotten back one positive response. *All* the schools that Warren had applied to had come back with positive responses.

Everyone wanted Warren.

And why not? Warren was everything a future doctor should be. Smart, kind, dedicated. Selfless.

Warren was everything that he hadn't been, Dan thought now with a sharp pang.

But he intended to be. He owed it to Warren to do the best job he could. Which was why his own plans, that of accepting NYU Hospital's lucrative offer to be one of their in-house radiologists, had been placed on hold for the next nine months. Possibly longer, although hopefully not. Only until the town found a doctor to take Warren's place.

Dan owed that much to Warren and this was one debt he intended to honor. Because, if not for him, Warren would be here right now, most likely staring down at the town that had happily greeted the news of his intentions of opening a practice here. No, Warren would be driving into the heart of this pint-size town, ready to roll up his sleeves and begin working right then and there.

And Forever would have been lucky to have him.

Warren was going to be the first doctor the town had had in decades. Currently, from what he'd managed to find out, if anyone became sick enough to need a doctor, he or she would have to drive to the next town, some fifty miles away.

He drew a deep breath as he continued to take in the surrounding terrain. It was one hell of a change from New York City. He was accustomed to having his choice of hospitals, to enjoying the company of an endless stream of physicians in all fields of expertise. Forever promised none of that. As far as he had determined, there was only one hospital in the region, and it was located in a place called Pine Ridge.

Which was why his brother had chosen Forever, Dan thought.

That was Warren. He never thought of himself or what he would miss out on by setting up a general practice in such an out-of-the-way place. All he ever thought about was how he could help. His brother had gone into medicine not for the money, not for the prestige but for the singular reason that he wanted to help his fellow human being, especially the ones who couldn't afford to help themselves.

And he'd been gone for almost a month.

"You're already probably a saint by now, making St. Peter feel humble just to be next to you," Dan murmured under his breath to the brother whose presence he could swear he still sometimes felt.

It was the middle of July and getting beyond hot, but he was in no hurry to drive into the town. He knew places like this existed, but he'd never been able to actually picture one. Hell, if he hadn't downloaded the latest maps onto his GPS, he doubted his ability to find the place. The whole area looked like an afterthought.

Afterthought.

Maybe that's what they should have named it, Dan thought. *Afterthought instead of Forever.*

"You lost, mister?"

The softly spoken question nearly caused Dan to jump out of his skin. When he swung around, not knowing who or what to expect, his heart raced.

He found himself looking at an olive complexioned

young man with the blackest hair he'd ever seen. It was peeking out from beneath an actual Stetson. The solemn-faced man wore a tan uniform with a sidearm strapped to his hip.

All in all the man looked as if he might have stepped out of the Old West—had it not been for the fact that the uniform looked clean and pressed. Instead of a horse, a Jeep stood parked in the background.

Dan thought of his own new car. A Jeep would have been a far more practical vehicle. But there had been a hundred details to see to, not to mention Warren's funeral service, so he'd let the ball drop in this one instance.

Dan found irony curving his mouth in response to the man's question about whether or not he was lost. He laughed shortly. "More than you can begin to guess, Sheriff."

"It's deputy," the young man corrected him. "Deputy Joe Lone Wolf. And if you tell me where you're headed, I can get you pointed in the right direction."

The right direction.

"That's a matter of opinion," Dan murmured more to himself than to the man standing beside him. "I'm due in Forever," he told the man who seemed to have the ability to move more silently than a shadow, "which I'm assuming is that collection of buildings just below us." He nodded toward the town.

"It is," Deputy Joe Lone Wolf verified. "Who is it in Forever who's expecting you?" he asked politely.

Dan took a deep breath and with it, he bid his former life goodbye and placed the life that would have been his present one on temporary hold. This was a promise he was determined to keep if he was ever to have a prayer of redemption.

Maybe, with luck, he wouldn't have to remain here for the entire nine months. Maybe someone else with Warren's noble mindset would come along and be dedicated to a place that looked as if it had barely scratched the surface of the twentieth century, much less the twenty-first.

Either a doctor like that, or one who would ultimately wash out in the real world. If the latter came along, the physician would be more than happy to practice in a place like Forever—one that couldn't afford to be choosy.

"My guess is most likely everybody," Dan said, answering the deputy's question about who was waiting to see him.

Joe frowned for a moment, as if far from pleased at the riddle the stranger had tossed at him. And then the light seemed to dawn on him. His somber face took on a whole different expression, softening as it did so. "You must be the new doc."

The term *new doc* would suggest that there was an *old doc* somewhere in this dusty, neglected place, Dan thought. He figured it was too much to hope for, but he asked anyway, "I was told that there were no doctors in Forever."

"There aren't," Joe confirmed. "According to Miss Joan, there was one in Forever once, but he died a long time ago."

Probably out of boredom, Dan thought, slanting another look at the place he was going to have to call home for the next three-quarters of a year. He kept the observation to himself.

Out loud, he asked, "Miss Joan?"

Joe nodded. "She runs the local diner. Miss Joan's been around here as long as anyone can remember. There's nothing worth knowing that Miss Joan doesn't know."

A town gossip, Dan thought. He knew the type. Someone to stay clear of.

As braced as he'd ever be, Dan extended his hand out and nodded at the man he guessed was going to be his guide into the heart of this Lilliputian-size village. "I'm Dr. Daniel Davenport."

"Daniel?" Joe echoed with a slight note of confusion. "They told me your first name was Warren."

"Warren's my brother." He realized he'd used the present tense, making the relationship an active, ongoing one. He hadn't gotten used to putting Warren into the past just yet. He knew he really didn't want to.

"Changed his mind and decided that he didn't want to practice in a small town after all, huh?" Joe guessed, nodding his head. "Can't say I don't understand," he went on before Dan could begin to explain the reason he was standing here instead of Warren. "Well, let's get you down there," Joe said, gesturing toward the town. "Got a lot of folks waiting on you."

Dan looked at the deputy in surprise. Was the man telling him that he had patients lining up already? This was clearly going to be his penance. Not that he didn't deserve it, Dan silently added. He deserved anything that was thrown at him.

"Exactly what do you mean by 'waiting on you'?" he asked.

In response, the deputy merely smiled. "You'll see," was all he said by way of an explanation.

It was going to be a long nine months, Dan thought as he got into his car and prepared to follow the deputy into Forever.

TINA BLAYNE COULDN'T remember ever seeing the diner this crowded before. There was barely any room in which to maneuver. Maybe she shouldn't have deliberately left coming to Miss Joan's diner for last. But then, that was the way she usually worked her way through the day.

Since she had gotten what she gratefully felt was a second chance here in this wonderful, tiny dot-on-the-map town less than a year ago, Tina had applied herself to the business of rebuilding her life and making something of herself so that she was able to provide for her eleven-month-old son, Bobby.

To that end, she'd taken those last three missing credits that allowed her to finally get her undergraduate degree. From there she'd begun work on her accounting degree, taking online classes whenever she could. She had a ways to go yet, but the point was that she *was* getting there and it felt as if everyone in Forever—not just her older sister, Olivia, and her brother-in-law, Rick, who also just happened to be the sheriff in Forever—was supporting her, cheering her on, pitching in when she needed help.

Why else would so many of the store owners suddenly turn to her to "help" them with their books? She knew that Miss Joan was behind that. The woman was certainly as sharp as they came and she could easily handle her own books, but Miss Joan had handed that off to her. Granted that the woman had her hands full, running the diner that was Forever's only decent place to eat, not to mention that it was also the last diner available for a good fifty miles to any traveler driving along the highway.

The latter fact was how she and Don, her son's father, had happened upon Forever, because they'd needed to stop for a meal. They'd also left Forever—and Bobby— in their rearview mirror the same day. She hadn't had much of a choice in that. It was during this sudden road trip that she'd realized Don was really, certifiably crazy And that, depending on his whim, he'd destroy all three of them.

She'd been too in love with Don in the beginning to see that. But she was well aware of it that day. And she'd turned out to be right. Don had tried to kill them both by driving his car into a tree.

Luckily, he'd only succeeded halfway. Don had died, she hadn't. And, after an emotionally rocky start, she finally began to live when she came out of her coma. That was all thanks to Olivia—and the caring, nurturing people of Forever.

As far as Tina was concerned, Forever was a perfect name for the place because she intended to stay here Forever, just like her older sister had. Moreover, this was the perfect place to raise her son—a place where everyone knew him and kept an eye out for him, just the way they kept an eye out for all the other children who lived here.

It didn't get any better than this, Tina thought. She supposed, in some people's opinion, it could be improved upon by introducing a little romance into her life, but she definitely didn't have time for that. Nor the inclination, either. Falling in love with the wrong man had almost ruined her life and had very nearly killed her.

As far as she was concerned, let the others, like Olivia and Mona, Rick's sister, have their romances. She'd had enough of so-called "romance" to last her a lifetime. Maybe two.

Walking through the diner, she hurried to the back before the tempting aroma of apple pie got to her and she stopped to have a piece. Nobody made apple pies like Miss Joan.

"Hey, wait up," Miss Joan called out just before she managed to reach the rear of the diner and the small, cluttered room that Miss Joan referred to as her "official" office.

Stopping, Tina turned around and glanced toward the owner of the diner. Miss Joan beckoned for her to come over, which she did.

"Where are you going?" Miss Joan asked.

Puzzled, Tina answered, "Your office. To do the books. The way I always do every Wednesday. Why?" She looked around again and spotted her sister and Rick at the far end of the diner. "Is something wrong?"

Rather than answer her question, Miss Joan responded with one of her own. "Did you forget?" The knowing look on the woman's face told her that she already had the answer to that one.

Tina thought for a moment, but couldn't come up with anything. "What is it that I forgot?" Tina asked.

Miss Joan gestured around toward the other occupants of the diner. The place got progressively crowded. It was three o'clock and although she always did a healthy business around lunchtime, this was past the normal lunch hour. At three the crowd should have thinned out considerably, remaining that way until business picked up again for dinner. But right now, there were no empty seats except one at the counter that Miss Joan had placed her own marker on, reserving it for someone.

Otherwise, the place was packed. The way it was whenever Miss Joan decided to throw a party and celebrate.

Was that what was going on?

It had been a hectic morning and for a second, Tina drew a complete blank. And then, just like that, it came back to her, a conversation she'd had with Miss Joan just last week. With her ninety-mile-an-hour life, she'd lost track of things again.

"Oh, that's right. The town's finally getting a doctor. Was that today?" Tina asked as she looked around the place again. She made eye contact with several people, who nodded in response.

Miss Joan came around from behind the counter and slipped a deceptively thin but strong arm around her shoulders.

"That's today," she confirmed, then clucked as she shook her head. "You've got too much on your mind these days, Baby Girl," the woman told her affectionately. "Being a mom to that handsome boy of yours, helping out your sister, doing the books for half the businesses in town. Pitching in here whenever one of the girls calls in sick and I'm shorthanded. Not to mention working on that accounting degree. You don't have time to sleep, much less have a little fun. No wonder that brain of yours is so overloaded. There's hardly any room in there for a new thought," Miss Joan lamented.

"You've gotta slow down before you burn the candle not just at both ends but down the middle, too," Miss Joan went on. "You don't have to do everything all at once. Learn how to kick back once in a while," the older woman advised.

"Now, sit yourself down," she coaxed, holding on to Tina's hand and leading her over to the stool she'd placed her sweater on earlier. She swept it off the seat, leaving it on the counter. "Have a little something to eat. Stay for the party." Miss Joan leveled a penetrating look at her, second-guessing the thoughts that were going through her head. "Those books in my office aren't going anywhere," she promised. "They'll still be there for you to go over in a couple of hours from now. Or even tomorrow if you can't get to them today."

The diner was her last stop of the day. It was here that Miss Joan and the waitresses took turns looking after her son while she worked. She felt good about that. Bobby certainly didn't lack for attention and she had no concerns about leaving him here. But in the end, the little boy was her responsibility and she needed to finish the books in order to be able to take care of him by the end of the day.

"But Bobby—"

"—is very happy where he is," Miss Joan assured her. To prove her point, she gestured toward the far end of the diner.

Bobby was playing with two of the waitresses. The women all took turns playing with him during their breaks and when there was a lull in business. Miss Joan pretended to look the other way. When it got busy, she took over caring for the boy. She made it seem completely effortless. It didn't hurt that the boy had taken to her from day one.

Any further protests that Tina might have had to offer were curtailed because, just then, the front door opened and Joe Lone Wolf walked in. He was followed in by another man.

Another man who was, just possibly, the most handsome-looking man Tina had ever seen in her life.

"Maybe I will stay for a few minutes," she heard herself telling Miss Joan as she sank down onto the last empty stool.

Her eyes were riveted on the town's first doctor in over three decades.

It took her a second to realize that her breath had backed up in her lungs.

Chapter Two

Dan silently scanned the interior of the diner. It was standing room only from what he could see. He couldn't help wondering if the entire town had piled into the aged, tarnished, silver railroad dining car wannabe, or if there were a few stray citizens who'd shown a little individuality, opted not to imitate sardines and had stayed away.

Despite how crowded it was, there were fewer people here than there had been in the last nightclub he'd been to. The last place he and Warren had been to, he amended, feeling the same sudden sharp pain in his gut that he did every time he thought of his late brother, which was still very, very often. He wondered if that would ever change, or at least get easier to bear.

Right now, from where he stood, he had serious doubts that it ever would.

Dan turned toward the deputy who had brought him to this place. "Is this everybody?" he asked, mildly curious.

His question brought a hint of amusement to the deputy's otherwise solemn face. "Just how little do you think Forever is?"

"Small," was all Dan said before he found himself on the receiving end of a surprisingly strong handshake delivered by a thin, ginger-haired woman of indeterminable age who had literally elbowed the deputy out of the way to get to him.

The woman had hazel eyes that seemed to go right through him, as deeply penetrating as any X-ray machine he'd ever encountered.

"Hello, I'm Joan Randall. Everyone around here just calls me Miss Joan." She made no attempt to hide the fact that she was looking him up and down as if he was a piece of merchandise. "So you're the new doctor," Miss Joan declared in a voice that was one part gravel, two parts aged Kentucky bourbon.

There was that word again, he thought. *New.* He banked down the urge to ask about the "old" doctor. They'd think he was being antagonistic, and he didn't mean to be. Ever since the fatal cab accident, he was having trouble finding a comfortable zone for his emotions. They kept flaring, bouncing all over the place, taking him with them.

He'd shift from sarcastic to contrite to cynical to humble. And sad, always sad, no matter what kind of front he put up. Coming here had been a duty, a responsibility he knew he had to shoulder. But *wanting* to be here was a whole different matter.

The woman who'd introduced herself as Miss Joan smiled at him. Her X-ray eyes smiled, as well. "Dr. Warren Davenport, right?" The X-ray eyes crinkled. "Welcome to Forever."

"It's Daniel," Dan corrected her. "Dr. Daniel Davenport."

A slight confused frown edged away the smile on the woman's thin lips. "I thought for sure they told me your first name was Warren," she said, referring to the people she'd spoken to on the phone in her quest to secure a physician for Forever.

It was through her efforts, as she relentlessly bombarded the American Medical Association with requests for a doctor, that Forever's situation, she'd been told, had come to Warren Davenport's attention. He'd been looking for some place where he could make a difference and Forever needed a dedicated doctor.

"Was there a mistake in the paperwork?" she now asked the young man before her.

The people in the diner seemed to tighten the circle around them. Dan doubted that it was just his imagination at work. Good thing for him that he wasn't claustrophobic, he thought.

"No, no mistake, Warren was supposed to be here. But there was an accident." He tried his best to sound detached as the words slowly left his lips. He had no intention of sharing his pain with anyone, least of all a town full of strangers.

"Was he badly hurt?" Miss Joan asked, concerned. He noticed that she still hadn't released his hand, although she had stopped pumping it.

His throat felt dry, scratchy, as he stoically replied, "He was killed."

"Oh." Miss Joan appeared genuinely stunned. "I'm sorry to hear that." He felt her squeeze his hand in what he assumed was a comforting gesture. "You've got the same last name. Was he a relative of yours?"

"He was my brother." Dan congratulated himself for not choking on his reply.

The woman's hazel eyes filled with compassion. The same look was mirrored in the eyes and faces of the people standing closest around him. For a moment, he was caught off guard.

Were they all pretending to be sympathetic?

After all, neither he nor his brother were anything to these people. Other than the obvious, that Warren was supposed to have come here to open up his practice, why would any of these people even care that he'd died? They'd never met Warren and as for him, well, they didn't know him from Adam. How could they pretend to know or feel his pain?

"I'm *really* sorry to hear that," Miss Joan murmured.

She sounded so sincere, he could almost believe that she meant it—if it didn't seem so impossible to him. She splayed her bony hand against her chest to emphasize what she was about to tell him.

"I'm the one who wrote to your brother. Actually," she amended, "I called and wrote letters to the AMA. They finally referred me to your brother." Her eyes met his and again, he had the eerie feeling that she could look right into him. "We only spoke the one time. But even then, he seemed like a very nice young man to me. Compassionate and caring," she added.

That described his brother to a T, Dan thought. Warren had been the good brother, he had been the wild one. And now, he thought heavily, he was the only brother. "He was."

Disappointment entered Miss Joan's voice. "You didn't have to come in person to deliver this news. I—we—would have understood."

Just for a second, Dan saw his way out of this prospective prison sentence. He could just nod, go along with the woman's interpretation of the situation and leave this speck of a place. Her assumption was his ticket back to New York. No one would be the wiser.

No one but him.

He'd made a promise. A promise to Warren that he would take his place until someone else more suitable could be found. Sure, he'd made the promise silently in his heart because Warren had been killed instantly when the taxi they were in had been slammed into by that swerving SUV.

But he wouldn't be able to look himself in the mirror each morning if he broke this promise to his dead brother.

Getting through each day was hard enough for him as it was. He couldn't shake off the mantle of blame for this, for Warren's death. If he hadn't prevailed on Warren and dragged him out—

This wasn't the time, Dan silently upbraided himself. The woman with the X-ray eyes would pick up on what he was thinking.

"I realize that," he said to the diner owner. "But I didn't come to tell you about my brother's untimely death. I came to Forever to take his place. Warren would have wanted me to," he felt obligated to add. He didn't want any of the people in town to be grateful to him. He didn't deserve gratitude.

The solemn mood that had begun to descend over the diner when they heard about Warren's death suddenly evaporated as Dan's words sank in.

Not one to leave anything to chance or misinterpretation, Miss Joan asked, "Then you're going to be our doctor?"

"Yes." He wanted to add that it was just until another substitute could be found, thereby giving himself the escape hatch he so badly needed. But something prevented him. Maybe he didn't want to leave himself open to endless attempts to persuade him to think otherwise. Or maybe, since they looked so happy to finally have a physician in their midst, he didn't want to be the one to rain on their parade.

Whatever the reason, for the time being he kept his qualifying phrase to himself.

The moment Miss Joan heard the word *yes,* the redhead's porcelain-fair face broke out in a huge smile that overtook her entire countenance.

"I see that selflessness runs in your family," she pronounced.

The last thing Dan wanted was to be regarded in the same light as Warren. They were nothing alike. Warren was the good one, the saint. The one who had entered medicine only with the thought of easing pain and giving back.

Dan began to deny Miss Joan's assumption—and to ask for the use of his hand back—but he never got the opportunity to do either.

Releasing her grip, the ginger-haired woman in the light gray and white waitress uniform managed to surprise him again by throwing her arms around him and enveloping him in a fierce bear hug.

"Welcome to Forever, Doc," she declared, a slight catch in her voice.

If he didn't know better, he would have said that he'd just crossed over to the other side, a place from which there was no return. As it was, an uneasy feeling rippled through him as Miss Joan continued to hug him, effectively pinning his arms to his sides. He didn't like being put up on a pedestal. It only made it that much easier for him to fall.

To his surprise, Miss Joan whispered something against his ear. "Any time you get the urge to just talk, feel free to come on by—day or night," she invited sympathetically.

For a moment he thought that this animated woman could sense that he didn't have anyone to talk to about Warren. At this point in their lives, he and his brother had no more family left. Uncle Jason had died two years ago, leaving his rather considerable bank accounts to them so that they could continue to fund their educations. Jason Davenport, their father's older brother, had taken them in when their parents had died in a plane crash fifteen years ago.

Now there was no family. And no girlfriend, neither his nor Warren's, in the wings ready to murmur sympathetic words. Warren had been so focused on becoming the best doctor he could, he never made time for a social life. As for him, he'd been too busy going from woman to woman to try to create even a semidecent relationship. Sure, he'd had a boatload of friends in college and during his residency, but the only one he had ever been remotely close to, *really* close to, was Warren.

Without commenting on Miss Joan's hushed offer, Dan separated himself from the woman only to find himself besieged by the people who had begun to close in on him when Miss Joan had first approached him. Without advanced warning, introductions suddenly came from all sides. People saying names he hadn't a prayer of remembering.

But he offered a perfunctory smile and nodded as if absorbing each and every one of them. In his place, he was certain that Warren *would* have remembered every single one. His brother had been like that. Warren had a knack for names and faces. Not only that, but he could zero in on the individuality of each person he came across.

As for him, well, he was better at remembering pretty women. And even then, it wasn't always a sure thing.

But this time, as names and greetings swirled around his head like bees swarming around a hive, while various people pumped his hand, Daniel found himself becoming progressively aware of the blonde in the background. She appeared to be quietly watching her friends and neighbors swirl around him. She seemed to have no desire to join in the swarming.

He was surprised that it had taken him this long to notice her. Rather than joining in the throng around him, she was perched on a stool at the counter, her body turned in his direction as if a detached observer to this little show.

Questions sprang up in his head even as he went on making automatic responses to the people around him.

Was she from around here?

He couldn't put his finger on it, but Dan had a feeling that maybe she wasn't.

Which brought up another question. Why would someone who wasn't born here willingly come to this little burg? Was it a matter of penance, the way it was for him? Or was there another reason the blonde had been transplanted?

As far as he could ascertain, there was no military base in the area, so she wasn't some serviceman's wife forced to temporarily call this forgotten part of the state her home.

What was her story?

As he pondered the question and debated how best to work his way over to the blonde, Dan suddenly found himself looking into the face of a man who had the easy air of assumed authority about him. The man had on the same kind of uniform as the deputy who had brought him to this place. Something told him that this man wasn't just another deputy.

And he was right. "I'm Sheriff Rick Santiago," the dark-haired man told him as he shook his hand. "You need anything, have any questions, come see me and I'll try to get you the answers and whatever else you might feel you need."

The offer was a friendly one, sincerely tendered.

There was no false air of bravado. What the sheriff said to him next cemented Dan's initial impression.

"Nobody expects you to remember all these names," Rick assured him. "It'll all come together for you after a while."

Dan forced a smile to his lips. He knew the sheriff meant well, but he had his doubts that he would remember half these names no matter how long he stayed here. And once he was back in New York, not just the names but the people as well would all become a vague blur to him in less than a week.

All except for the blonde, he amended.

The blonde had the kind of face and body that lingered on a man's mind long after she was physically gone from the room. That would be especially true if they interacted before he left Forever.

Miss Joan seemed to read his mind. He hadn't realized that she was still this close by.

Before he knew it, the woman had slipped her arm through his and drew him over closer to where the blonde was sitting at the counter.

"That's Tina Blayne, the sheriff's sister-in-law." Turning her face so that only he could see her smile and hear what she had to tell him, she said, "You'll probably be seeing a lot of her."

Now how the hell did the woman know that? He looked at her, banking down his curiosity and only looking mildly interested in what Miss Joan was saying.

"Oh?"

Miss Joan nodded. "Yeah. Because of her little boy, Bobby. Cute as all get-out, but he keeps coming down with colds and fevers. She's been running herself ragged, driving over to Pine Ridge every time the poor kid's fever spikes. That, on top of working and taking classes for her degree, has been taking quite a toll on her. She's really relieved about you—your brother—a doctor," she finally settled on, "coming to town. Maybe the poor thing'll get some sleep now." She gestured toward the blonde she'd referred to as Tina, beckoning her over. "C'mere, Tina. Meet the new doc," she coaxed.

Tina had been sitting there, observing from a distance, thinking to herself that the man who had arrived was just too damn good-looking to be much of a doctor. He looked like Hollywood's concept of a doctor, not the real thing.

If the man actually had a degree, she had a feeling that he hadn't really earned it. Most likely he'd gotten it by cutting corners. Men who looked like that always cut corners. Always used their good looks and charm to get by. They didn't have to be good, they just had to smile and sound as if they knew what they were talking about.

She was well versed in the ways—and shortcomings—of good-looking men. Don had belonged to that club and if she hadn't had the strength of character, a good-looking man would have been her downfall, if not her complete demise.

But, after Olivia, Miss Joan was like a second mother to her. It was Miss Joan who insisted she and Bobby come live with her once Olivia had gotten married to Rick. Miss Joan was also the one who had encouraged her to continue her education online. Once she was on that path, Miss Joan had urged her friends to take her on as an accountant even though her degree and accreditation were still more than a few months in the future.

So, when Miss Joan wanted her to go some place or be somewhere, she was not about to say no to the woman. Even if she would have preferred to beg off. This was Miss Joan and she'd walk through fire for the woman, she was that grateful to her.

Tina slid off the stool and approached the gathering around the new doctor. Miss Joan deliberately signaled for several of the men to step aside and clear a path for Tina. No one said no or ignored Miss Joan. They knew better than that.

"Dr. Daniel, this is Tina Blayne," Miss Joan said, resting her hands on Tina's slim shoulders. The next moment, she delicately pushed Tina in closer to the town's new addition. "I have a feeling the two of you will be seeing a lot of each other," she pronounced.

Tina looked at the woman sharply.

Miss Joan smiled innocently, as if she had said nothing out of the ordinary. Certainly nothing that Tina should find upsetting.

"I told him about Bobby and how sick he's been lately," Miss Joan explained after a sufficient beat had gone by.

Well, Dan decided, he might not want to be here and was here pretty much under duress—even if it was of his own making. But he was a doctor and he liked to think that he was a damn decent one, even if he hadn't exactly graduated at the top of his class. That outcome had been not because he didn't know his material, or because he wasn't skilled at his craft. It was because he'd preferred partying to working on imaginary patients and cadavers. But when it came to the real thing, he was as conscientious as they came.

"Bobby?" he asked. She'd just said the name to him a couple of minutes ago. Referring to who? His brain still felt as if it was throbbing.

"My son," Tina told him.

"Right." He had to get his act together. Miss Joan had just told him that, Dan thought. He glanced at the young mother's left hand. It was devoid of any rings. Divorced? Widowed? In any event, he took the absence of a ring to mean that she was a single mother. Things became interesting again.

"Why don't you bring him by my office?" Dan told her. "Once I have an office," he qualified.

"Oh, you have an office," Miss Joan assured him. "Once you unwind a little I'm sure that the sheriff'll be glad to take you there. Right, Rick?" she asked, peering around the new doctor's arm.

"Just say when," Rick replied good-naturedly.

"He will," Miss Joan promised in Dan's stead. She turned her attention back to the guest of honor. "But right now—" she looked around at the faces of the people she had, for the most part, watched grow up over the years, and then loudly declared "—we're going to welcome ourselves a doctor."

"About time!" a burly man toward the front of the crowd called out.

Miss Joan laughed and nodded. "I couldn't agree with you more, Ezra." She glanced over her shoulder toward two of her waitresses. "Julie, Rosa, see that everyone has a glass—and be sure to fill it. We need to make a toast to Dr. Dan."

Dan braced himself for whatever was ultimately coming. He didn't mind being in the spotlight, but he had the feeling that this attention came with a great many strings. He had one hell of a challenge in front of him.

This toast's for you, Warren, Dan thought. *Not me.* He knew his brother would have been moved by it. As for him, it just gave him a feeling of anticipation that was far from good.

He sincerely hoped that he was up to the challenge. For Warren's sake, he was going to have to be.

Chapter Three

"To Doctor Dan!" Miss Joan toasted with enthusiasm, raising her glass of sparkling cider high. "Thanks for setting up your practice here and we all hope that you never come to regret it."

Dan raised his own glass to his lips. The woman was asking a great deal. More than was possible. If this was only about him, he'd be already regretting it. Already booking a flight back.

But this wasn't about what he wanted. It was about Warren and what he had wanted. What he *selflessly* had wanted.

For now, he would make the best of it and muster through.

As the light amber liquid made its way past his lips and down his throat, the taste created a note of confusion in its wake. He'd thought that the waitresses had poured some sort of alcoholic beverage into the glasses that they then distributed to him and the others. One taste negated that impression. Other than a few bubbles and a deceptively yellowish color, what had been poured into his glass fell woefully short of having any sort of a kick.

His drink tasted suspiciously like soda pop.

Dan regarded his glass, unconsciously raising a quizzical eyebrow as he tried to pinpoint just what it was he was drinking.

Seeing his confused expression, Tina leaned into him so he could hear her. "It's sparkling cider," she told him, then added, "this is a diner. Miss Joan doesn't serve any hard liquor here."

For a moment, he was distracted by Tina's closeness and the scent of her hair. Something light and floral. And heady.

Dan forced himself to focus on the conversation. Okay, no hard liquor. He could deal with that. But no liquor at all was something else again.

He thought of wine. Entire cultures had wine with their dinner. Dan sincerely hoped that this wasn't a dry town. "How about 'soft' liquor?"

Amusement entered her eyes at the term. "None of that, either."

"Do they have any liquor at all in this town?"

He wasn't addicted to drinking, but he wanted to know if it was available should the need arise. There were times, since Warren's death, that he felt the need to numb himself against the haunting memory of Warren's last cry of pain and surprise. And, now that he thought of it, a drink at the end of the day after dealing with the good citizens of Sleepy Hollow might not be such a bad idea, either.

"You can find some in Hogan's General Store," she

told him, giving him the name of the biggest grocery store/pharmacy in Forever. "Mostly, Mr. Hogan sells beer, but if you catch him in a good mood, he'll take you to where he keeps the top shelf stuff. Whiskey, vodka, whatever your pleasure," she told him.

Tina was doing her best not to prejudge the new doctor, or sound judgmental. But Don had been a drinker, as well as a closet drug addict. At the time she'd thrown her lot in with his, it hadn't mattered. She'd been desperate to connect with someone other than the sister who had assumed the role of both mother and father to her. But it mattered now.

Looking back, she realized now that Olivia had worked incredibly challenging hours just to provide for them as well as furthering her law career. But at the time all she could think of was that her sister was never physically there when she wanted her. And Don might have ultimately been a very poor excuse for a human being, but he had been incredibly charismatic when he wanted to be. She had been both lonely and highly impressionable when their paths crossed.

In essence, she supposed she was a victim waiting to happen. But she survived all that, Tina thought, struggling to focus on the positive the way she'd learned to do. Survived, was the stronger for it and had a beautiful son to boot. All the rest of it was in the past and no longer of any consequence.

Since Miss Joan had personally placed a glass of sparkling cider in her hand, Tina raised it now a beat after the others had chanted the toast to the doctor. The pause was part of her effort not to just blindly follow someone else's lead, even if that someone was Miss Joan. It was all part of the evolution she was determined to go through.

"To your stay in Forever," she said, altering the toast to something she felt was more appropriate. Dr. Daniel Davenport didn't have the air of someone who belonged in Forever.

Because of the din, Dan was forced to watch the sexy blonde's lips to "hear" what she was saying.

Not exactly a hardship, he mused, since her lips were full and, at any other time, would have been decidedly tempting. But he wasn't himself these days. He still struggled with his grief and the almost oppressively heavy weight of guilt that pressed down on him. Each time he managed to come up for air, to begin to pull himself together, the guilt would suddenly find him, stealing away the very air in his lungs.

Six weeks after Warren's death he was still caught in an emotional tailspin. A small part of him was the old Dan, the man he'd been before Warren had died because of him. The rest was a pulsating, formless glob of sadness and guilt, viewing everything around him in shades of gray and black.

The first part was mired in denial. The second part was just mired. Both parts, he felt now, would need something stiffer than what was in his glass.

"This is Texas," he pointed out needlessly to the shapely blonde. "Aren't there any bars or saloons or whatever the locals call them around here?"

She noticed that he said "the locals," not "you locals." Was he deliberately excluding her from being part of

Forever, giving her what he must have assumed was a compliment? Or was that just a slip of the tongue that he wasn't aware of?

"There's a place on the other side of town," she told him. "It's called 'The Cattlemen.'" The entire building was hardly big enough to be able to sustain the sign that proclaimed its name, but it did qualify for the label of *saloon*.

"Didn't think that this town was big enough to have an other side," the doctor quipped.

That was a definite put-down. Tina took offense for her adopted town. But when she looked at Forever's newest resident, she didn't see a smug, superior expression on his face. Instead, his expression appeared unfathomable, as if his heart and mind were elsewhere and his mouth just moved thanks to some automatic pilot setting.

"It is and it does," she assured him. She gave him a rundown on the establishment's hours of operation. "The Cattlemen is only open after seven. The man who runs it also owns the barbershop next door and he works there in the daytime."

"After seven," Dan repeated incredulously, thinking of the bars and grills located on practically every other corner back in three of New York City's five boroughs. Most of those establishments opened before noon under the guise of serving lunch. "How long does this Cattlemen stay open?"

Her eyes met his. *Was* the new doctor a closet drinker? she wondered uneasily.

Her expression gave nothing away as she answered, "Long enough."

Her response brought an amused smile to his lips. The blonde probably thought he had a drinking problem. Nothing could be further from the truth. He had absolutely no intentions of drowning himself at the bottom of a bottle. For one thing, it wasn't a solution. Warren still wouldn't be alive once he sobered up. He was here, in Forever, for Warren's sake. To make it up to his brother, at least a little—if Warren was up there somewhere, looking down and watching.

He vacillated between believing in an afterlife and cynically regarding it as a myth intended to give people something to hold on to during the worst spates of their lives. Today he found himself somewhere on middle ground. Mostly he was just hoping to get through this without embarrassing his brother's memory.

"YOU LOOK LIKE THE CAT that swallowed a whole pitcher of cream," Sheriff Rick Santiago observed as he passed Miss Joan in another part of the diner. He stopped to study the woman who had been one of his late grandmother's friends. "What are you up to?" he asked. A hint of amusement flared in his green eyes as he regarded the owner of the diner.

Instead of answering the sheriff directly, Miss Joan nodded toward where the new doctor and Rick's sister-in-law were standing at the counter.

"What do you see?" she asked, her voice deliberately innocent.

Rick glanced in the general direction the woman

indicated. But he was accustomed to taking in the bigger picture. "A damn good tally for you at the end of the day."

Miss Joan's throaty laugh rumbled between them for a moment. "Well, yeah, there's that, too, but something more interesting is going on. Look again."

He narrowed his field of reference and went with the obvious. "We've finally gotten a doctor to practice in this one-horse town."

"To go with the lawyer you got last year," Olivia chimed in, joining her husband and Miss Joan. As Rick slipped his hand around her waist, drawing her closer, Olivia leaned her head against his shoulder. She was the picture of contentment—as well as pregnancy. "I won't have a fifty-mile trip in front of me when my water breaks," she said gratefully. "Looks like civilization has finally come to Forever," she declared, immensely pleased.

"Looks like more than that from where I'm standing," Miss Joan propped.

This time Rick and Olivia both looked over toward the diner owner's reference point.

"Tina's talking to the new doctor," Olivia noted. That seemed only natural, considering that Bobby'd had more than his share of earaches and colds this past winter. Tina doted on the boy. Most likely, she was telling the new doctor all about him.

This could go on all afternoon, Miss Joan thought. Deciding to call an end to the fruitless guessing game, she gave them the answer she was waiting for.

"Tina's also smiling wider than I've ever seen her smile," Miss Joan pointed out.

Olivia narrowed her eyes a little, staring more intently at her sister. So that was it. Miss Joan was playing matchmaker. Well, the woman had certainly picked the wrong target this time.

"If you're trying to pick out a man for my sister, I really wouldn't get my hopes up if I were you."

Miss Joan had had several husbands in her lifetime. Three by some people's count, four by others. And it was rumored that there had also been a number of serious love affairs when she'd been a very young woman. Unattached at present, the woman was nonetheless a romantic at heart and believed that men and women were created solely for the purpose of being paired up.

"Why not?" she asked, her eyes pinning Olivia in place. "Tina's a young, pretty girl with her head on straight, and in case you haven't noticed because you only seem to have eyes for Rick here, that new doc's real easy on the eyes."

Olivia shook her head. "That's just the problem," she informed the older woman.

Miss Joan looked at her for a long moment, clearly confused. "His being easy on the eyes?" she asked, unable to make any sense out of Olivia's response.

"No, his being good-looking," Olivia specified. She could see that Miss Joan wasn't following this line of thinking so she made it clear for the woman. "The guy who almost ended my sister's life—and who wanted to have their son die with them—was one of the handsomest specimens of manhood ever created. He was downright beautiful," she concluded.

In that he was very much like the fallen angel, Lucifer, Olivia couldn't help adding silently. And her sister had fallen for the worthless piece of wasted flesh like the proverbial ton of bricks. Tina had almost paid for her mistake with her life.

"More beautiful than me?" Rick asked teasingly.

She turned her body in toward him, brushing against him and creating a sizzle between them. She put her hand against his cheek, all the love she felt shining in her eyes. "I hate to tell you this, Rick, but you're not beautiful. You, Sheriff Santiago, are ruggedly handsome. Especially when you come to bed with your badge pinned to your naked chest," she added with a laugh, punctuating her declaration with a quick kiss.

"Now *that* I'd like to see," Miss Joan hooted.

"No offense, Miss Joan," Olivia told the woman for whom she bore a great deal of affection, "but that's never going to happen." Her eyes danced as she specified, "That's for private showings only."

Miss Joan laughed, her low, Kentucky bourbon voice rumbling mildly. It pleased her more than she could say that Rick had finally found someone who could love him the way he fully deserved to be loved. He'd gone through a lot in his life, not the least of which was magnanimously reconciling with the mother who had abandoned him when he was a kid and his sister had been a year-old baby.

His sister had gone through the same set of hard knocks, in addition to stubbornly resisting the obvious.

Luckily, Mona had finally come to her senses and was now engaged to Joe Lone Wolf, the deputy who had loved her from the first moment he'd laid eyes on her all the way back in grade school.

Forever looked forward to celebrating another wedding. Who knew? the woman silently speculated. There might be two in the offing. She had a great deal of affection in her heart for both Tina and her son. They currently lived with her, and while she was content to let the situation continue indefinitely, she knew that wasn't in the best interest of the girl. Tina needed to have someone in her life to love, someone who loved her back the way she should be loved.

From where she stood, that man could very well be Dr. Dan.

"I can respect that," Miss Joan said to Olivia. The statement was followed by a broad wink which told the sheriff's wife that while she might have gotten a few years on her now, beneath it all was still the heart of a lusty, raring-to-go young woman who enjoyed the more physical side of love just as much as she enjoyed the concept of love in general.

Maybe even a little more.

Olivia read between the lines and made an accurate assessment. "Never mind my sister," she said to the diner owner. "I think we're going to have to find you a man, Miss Joan."

Rather than protest that she didn't know what she was talking about, or silently waving away the notion, Miss Joan treated them both to another wide, and this time unabashedly lusty, grin.

"Well, if you find someone who can keep up with me, Olivia, you know where to bring him. My door's always open."

Rick laughed softly. Leaning into his wife, he whispered so that only Olivia could hear him. "My guess is that's not the only thing that's ope— Hey!" he cried in surprise as Olivia swatted at him to keep him from finishing his sentence.

"Hush," Olivia chided, a warning look in her eyes.

It wasn't that she was afraid the older woman would take offense. It was just that she didn't want her going off on a bawdy tangent the way she knew Miss Joan was very capable of doing.

Out of hearing range because of the increasing din, Miss Joan laughed at Olivia's quick movement to silence her husband.

She guessed at the reason behind Olivia's actions. She'd come to know both sisters very well since they'd arrived in Forever.

"Whatever he was about to say, Livy, I've heard ten times worse. My second husband, Bill, flew on helicopter missions. He was a tail gunner in Vietnam during the war. They haven't invented a cuss word that didn't come out of Bill's mouth at one time or another." She paused a moment. "Come to think of it, Bill wasn't all that different from my first husband, Ray."

Putting her memories behind her, Miss Joan shifted her attention to the present and the reason that her diner was filled to overflowing.

"Well, it looks like everybody's here who's going to be here," she decided, then announced to the sheriff and his wife, as well as to several people who could actually hear her without her resorting to a microphone, "That means it's time to bring out the cake."

"Cake?" Alma Sanchez, one of Rick's other deputies piped up, coming closer to her boss and the diner owner. For a woman who had a continuing love affair with all manner of sweets, with pastries at the top of the list, Deputy Alma Sanchez was an exceedingly petite, trim woman. "Did someone say cake?"

"Of course I said cake," Miss Joan underscored. "You can't expect to welcome someone properly without having baked a cake in his honor."

The diner owner's hazel eyes darted back and forth, taking Rick into account and then zeroing in on Joe, another young boy she'd watched grow to manhood, fulfilling the promise he'd projected years ago. She had no children of her own, but viewed so many of the town's younger citizens as her own.

Joe was standing a few feet away, talking to his fiancée. She needed to borrow him for a few minutes. "Rick, Joe," she called, raising her voice, "I need a couple of men with strong backs."

"Thinking of taking them back to your place, Joan?" Mac Tyler called out, laughing at the joke he thought he'd just made.

"Better them than you, Mac, that's for sure," Miss Joan fired back without missing a beat. "If that man's ego was any bigger," Miss Joan confided to Olivia in tones that were not as hushed as they could have been, "he wouldn't be able to get his head through a single doorway."

Mac Tyler had also been sniffing at her heels for the longest time and at this stage of her life, she still hadn't made up her mind if she wanted to make something of it or not. She couldn't decide if Tyler was worth the trouble or the effort.

"C'mon, boys," Miss Joan gestured to the sheriff and his senior deputy, "I've got a cake I need you to bring out of the walk-in." Glancing over her shoulder, she addressed her words to the people in the diner. "Nobody even *think* about making a move toward the door. I'm bringing out the cake."

Appreciative murmurs greeted her declaration. Everyone knew that Miss Joan's cakes were conceived in heaven and given an earthly form as an afterthought. Rick's late grandmother, a woman not easily given to offering compliments, had once asked Miss Joan how she kept her cakes from floating away.

As Miss Joan left the room, leading the way for her two helpers, Dan turned to Tina and asked, "She always take charge like that?"

There was more than a little affection in her expression as Tina's mouth curved. "Actually, this is one of Miss Joan's more laid-back days," she said with an amused laugh.

Dan hardly heard her answer. The din in the diner had swallowed them up without so much as a telltale trace. He was forced to watch her mouth again in order to hear what she'd said.

He didn't really mind.

Chapter Four

"This is it?"

Disbelief permeated Dan's every syllable. It was a struggle not to allow his mouth to drop open in sheer, stunned amazement.

What the hell did I just get myself into?

That was his initial reaction to the two-story, ramshackle seventy-five-year-old building that was to serve as both his home and the medical clinic. The ground floor was devoted to a couple of exam rooms, an office he could barely stretch out in and a reception area. The second floor was where the last doctor had lived thirty years ago.

Joe had once again volunteered to be his guide and had brought him here, leading the way in his Jeep, after the welcoming party had wound down. When the deputy had come to a stop before this building, Dan had followed suit. He'd gotten out of his sedan in what felt like surreal slow motion. His eyes were riveted to the dark, inhospitable and, undoubtedly, rotting building.

Dan felt like someone trapped in a nightmare he could only hope would end quickly. Except that it showed no signs of ending any time soon. The building loomed before him like a refugee from a bad, grade B, 1950s horror movie. All that was needed were bats.

Joe shifted ever so slightly, picking up on the other man's disbelief. In comparison to what he'd known, the old building was in good condition.

"Yeah, this is it," Joe acknowledged.

Still stunned, Dan turned to the deputy. Maybe this was some kind of a hazing, a prank the town was playing on "the new guy." How was he supposed to work with this? The place probably leaked when it rained. And if it looked like this on the outside, what did it look like inside? What kind of equipment would he find?

Would he find equipment?

"You're kidding," he said to Joe, in fervent hopes that the stoic man had a warped sense of humor.

Joe's tone was low, soft. Soothing. "It doesn't look like much now—"

Now, there was a world-class understatement. "Did it ever?" Dan asked, cutting in.

How the hell was he supposed to work in a place like this, much less live in it?

Granted, he was accustomed to places like his late uncle's spacious house in the Hamptons or the Fifth Avenue apartment that he and Warren had shared during their residency at NYU. Maybe that might have made him a snob in some people's eyes. But there had to be a happy medium between where he'd come from and this.

The place looked hardly worthy of the label Rundown Shack. He had strong suspicions a massive collection of termites holding hands kept the walls up. If they ever let go, the walls, not like at Jericho, would come tumbling down without any kind of a warning.

He recalled that Warren had seen photographs of the place. The diner woman, Miss Jane or Joan or some name that began with a *J*, had sent them to him. His brother had never showed the photos to him, but he'd been excited about "the possibilities."

The only possibility Dan saw was if the house was knocked down and someone started from scratch. And even then, he wasn't so sure.

How could Warren have willingly agreed to live in this house? In this town? There was dedication and then there was insanity.

"Yeah," Joe answered his question about what the building had looked like once. "It did. And with a little work," he maintained rather firmly, "it can look that way again."

He'd obviously insulted the man's sense of loyalty to his place of birth, Dan thought. And he hadn't meant to, but, hell, hopeless was hopeless. And this was hopeless.

"Define *a little*," Dan muttered under his breath.

"Okay," Joe allowed reluctantly, "maybe a lot of work. But compared to the place I grew up in, this house looks pretty decent."

"You grew up in a homeless camp?" The quip was out before Dan could think better of it.

The solemn man was quiet for a long moment. But it was clear that Joe had taken no offense as he replied, "Almost."

The deputy sounded so serious Dan instantly regretted the offhanded remark. He hadn't wanted to be disparaging. People were saddled with poverty through no fault of their own. He'd never been, but he and Warren had been two of the lucky ones—at the time, he amended. Until Warren's luck had run out.

He could feel his gut twisting.

He'd never been good at apologizing, but he gave it a shot. "Hey, I'm sorry, man. I didn't mean to—"

Joe held his hand up as if to push any further apologetic words away. "That's okay. I grew up on the reservation. It's not all that far from the other side of town," Joe added in case the doctor was unaware that there was a reservation in the area.

What Joe didn't bother touching on was any of his history, or the fact that he'd been orphaned at an early age and raised by a more or less disinterested committee of distant relatives, all of whom had felt he was someone else's responsibility.

"Things turned out okay." He turned to look at Dan. "And you might not think so now, but this will, too. Things have a habit of turning out around here," he assured Dan.

Dan sighed, looking at the building again. He hadn't come here for a vacation, he reminded himself. This was all part of the penance he felt he had to undertake.

He frowned, his eyes sweeping over the structure. No question he would have to find a better place to attend to the patients lining up to see him—and soon. The inside of that building was a breeding ground for every bacteria known—and unknown—to man.

What had Warren been thinking when he'd agreed to put down a bid on this place?

A bid.

Dan found the term humorous. A bid would indicate that some sort of competition to secure this pathetic house/office. Who in their right mind would *want* this place?

Warren. Maybe his brother had seen something here that he wasn't seeing, Dan speculated. But then, Warren had always been the one to bring home strays and try to mend their broken limbs as well as their broken spirits. This place certainly qualified for that. If ever he'd seen anything broken, this house was it.

First thing tomorrow, he would get on the phone with some local contractors to make this place inhabitable. Since he'd seen no sign of a hotel in the area, he supposed he would have to rough it for tonight.

He fervently hoped that there was at least running water in the place, but he wasn't about to place any bets. Bracing himself, he walked up onto the wooden front porch. The moment he did, he heard the wood groan beneath his shoes. It continued to groan with each step he took.

Joe glanced down at the offending slats. "That might need fixing," he suggested.

Dan deliberately looked down at the boards beneath his feet. "Good guess," he cracked.

The front door was ajar, with just enough space between it and the doorjamb to allow a medium-size furry invader to slip in. The thought did little to warm Dan's heart.

Hand on the doorknob, Dan tried it and found that neither the doorknob nor the door would budge.

"Here," Joe offered, politely edging him out of the way and placing his own torso in front of the offending door. "You don't want to risk hurting that shoulder of yours."

"And you can?" Dan asked.

"Part of the job," was all Joe said.

Anything else he might have said in response died away as both he and Dan became aware of the sound of vehicles approaching in the distance. Dan turned from the house to see several cars, Jeeps mostly, but there was a truck or two as well, coming closer. Was it starting already?

"They don't give you much time to set up here, do they?" he asked the deputy.

Well, whatever their complaints were, unless it pertained to a heart attack or a gunshot wound, the good citizens of One-Horse Town were going to have to wait until he had a chance to settle in and get the medical office in some kind of working order. He had his medical bag with him but he had a feeling that he would need a lot more in his supply closet before he could consider the place up and running.

Joe made no attempt to answer him. Instead, the deputy left his side and walked up to the first vehicle. He shouted out several names, greeting the people who were now disembarking, spilling out onto the front yard like the inhabitants of a circus clown car.

And every single one of them, man, woman and child alike, carried tools.

Confused, Dan looked to Joe for an explanation, but the deputy had moved on and was now busy, talking to a slender, dark-haired young woman with a quick smile and green flashing eyes. Dan didn't remember seeing her at the diner. Probably couldn't wiggle her way in, he speculated. The place had been crowded beyond belief by the time he and Joe had left.

And now they were all here. Why they had come with tools, he couldn't begin to fathom—unless they were looking to barter, trading an item they thought he might need or want in exchange for his medical services.

He was fairly certain he was right. It felt like that kind of a place. A throwback to a simpler time.

Dan made up his mind to address his patients en masse. It saved time. "I can't see any of you until I've had a chance to sanitize the exam room." *Assuming that's even possible.* He might just be taking things for granted.

"That's why we're here, Doc," the sheriff told him, making his way to the front of the gathering. "We thought an extra pair of hands—or seven—might just help that along as bit."

Burning the building down to the ground and starting from scratch would help even more. But Dan thought it wise to keep that observation to himself.

Instead, he saw more vehicles approaching on the horizon. "Looks like more than just a couple of extra pairs of hands to me."

The sheriff flashed a grin as he inclined his head in agreement. "Math was never my strong suit. C'mon," he urged, "let's see how bad it really is."

One hand holding on to a rather massive toolbox, Rick placed another hand on Dan's shoulder, acting as if they were old friends instead of two men who'd met only a couple of hours ago.

As the sheriff urged him into the house, with Joe and a man who'd introduced himself earlier as Mick Henley, the town mechanic, bringing up the rear, Dan saw yet another vehicle pull up in front of the house. Tina, the blonde he'd talked to at the diner, and the sheriff's wife, Olivia, got out. Between them, the women were carrying a rather large, unwieldy cooler.

"Miss Joan thought you might need this," Olivia said, addressing her words to her husband.

Dan thought he'd heard the sound of glass clanking against glass. "More sparkling cider?" he guessed.

Tina smiled. Setting the cooler down on the grass, she threw back the cooler top for a moment and revealed bottles of beer tightly nestled together on mounds of shaved ice.

"Guess again," she suggested.

Dan looked down into the cooler, perplexed. "I thought you said that she didn't have anything stronger than cider."

"She doesn't believe in serving liquor of any kind at the diner. But this is another kind of a situation and Miss Joan is a woman of many resources," Rick informed him. He glanced around at the crowd. Everyone who'd said they were coming appeared to be here. "You ready to get started?" he asked.

Dan pressed his lips together. Actually, he wasn't. He

just wanted to stretch out for a while and let the reality of the turn his life had taken have a chance to set in.

But to say so didn't seem right, not with all these people gathering around the place, wielding various tools, intent on rebuilding everything. They were obviously determined to take a sow's ear and make, if not a silk purse, then at least a better sow's ear, out of what they found before them.

Taking a breath, he nodded. "Ready," Dan acknowledged.

The sheriff led the way. Dan followed him into the house. The interior was oppressively dark, with the bright daylight outside only managing to wiggle in here and there, casting pinpricks of illumination that somehow managed to make the house seem darker and more gloomy, not less.

The inside of the house looked more like a medieval prison cell than a place of potential healing. Dan hadn't a clue where to begin, how to get started.

It took him a second to realize that he didn't have to know how to get started renovating his new home. Behind him, he heard Tina organizing the women, breaking them down into smaller groups and assigning them to different areas. He'd never heard a drill sergeant with a soft voice before.

"Lucinda, Rachel, Claire, you're with Olivia. Go upstairs and get started on the two bedrooms. Becky, Allyson, Rosa, you're with me. Let's tackle the kitchen first and leave the men to see what needs fixing or rebuilding."

The next moment, he was aware of the clatter of

buckets, mops and bottles of cleaning products rubbing against one another as they were carried off to various destinations within the dank-looking house.

Within minutes of the group's arrival, Dan found himself working with the sheriff and the town's only car mechanic, replacing the sections of rotting drywall that had been uncovered in the kitchen.

If either man noticed his severe lack of expertise, neither of them made any mention of it. Instead, Rick scaled back his initial instructions to him. The man took over the bulk of the work, using the same excuse that Joe had used when the deputy had urged him not to attempt to push open the door on his own. Rick overruled his protest by telling him that he couldn't risk doing any damage to himself.

"Especially not to your hands," Rick pointed out. "You get hurt and then all of this will be for no reason," he added, nodding toward the different clusters of people who were now busy working on the ground floor of the house.

From the sounds Dan heard overhead, more people were doing the same upstairs. He hadn't even been up there to see what they were up against, but he had a feeling that it was more of the same—if not worse.

"Town's been waiting for a doctor for thirty years. Wouldn't seem right letting you run the chance of getting hurt your first day here," Rick told him, taking another pass over the newly installed drywall—how had he done it so fast?—with his trowel. The sheriff flashed a grin at Dan. "We want you to like the place."

He wondered what the man would say if he knew

that whether or not he *liked* the town had nothing to do with his remaining here. He decided it only fair to set the sheriff's mind at ease.

"Don't worry about that," Dan told him. "I'm not about to leave."

Tina was standing right behind the doctor when he said that. She wondered if it was her imagination, or if anyone else thought that the man sounded very solemn—perhaps even sad—when he assured her brother-in-law that he wasn't going anywhere. She'd heard Dan talking earlier, when he'd told Miss Joan that, in coming here, he was taking his late brother's place.

What was the story behind that? she couldn't help wondering.

Ever since she'd moved here with her son and her sister, she'd found herself taking a far greater interest in people, in their lives, than she ever had before. She was fascinated by what caused them to make certain choices in their lives.

Well, she decided, when Daniel Davenport was ready, he'd tell people the backstory behind the reason he was here. Until then, she was content with speculating. It made life interesting.

"Ready for a beer?" Tina asked as she made her way into the center of the three men. She was carrying four bottles of beer nestled in her arms and without waiting for an answer, began distributing them. The last bottle she took for herself.

"Thanks," Dan said.

He wiped the sweat from his brow with the back of his wrist. He hadn't been aware until this moment just how tired, sweaty—and thirsty—he was. Twisting the cap off, he took a long swig from the bottle. Dan couldn't remember when he'd had something that tasted this good. He couldn't remember the last time he'd actually had to physically exert himself. Undoubtedly he would pay for this. He could feel his muscles already aching.

He realized that Tina was about to walk away and dug deep for the words to say so that she would linger a moment longer. "I don't see Miss Joan around."

Tina smiled. Pausing, she broke the seal on her bottle, twisted off the cap and took a sip. "That's because she's not."

"Why? I would have thought something like this was right up her alley. Holding court, ordering people around," he added when Tina made no comment.

"Someone had to stay behind and run the diner. People are always passing through. In the meantime, they're hungry and thirsty. Besides, she volunteered to take care of Bobby so I could help out here."

She'd mentioned the name before, but he couldn't remember in what context. "Bobby," he repeated, hoping she would take the hint and embellish.

Tina nodded. "My son," she told him just before she tipped the bottle back and took a longer swig from it. "You're going to have to work on your memory skills, Doctor," she commented.

He nodded. "I'll put it on my to-do list," he promised.

Dan suddenly realized that he was flirting with her. Wow. He hadn't thought he was capable, given his present state of mind. Was that a hopeful sign? Or was he just on automatic pilot, responding to a given situation the way he always had before?

The next moment, someone was calling Tina away.

"Got more drywall to replace, Doc," Joe called out to him.

"Coming," he responded, setting his bottle down. He needed to be kept busy, Dan thought, looking over his shoulder at Tina. For more reasons than one.

Chapter Five

"Why?"

Dan asked the question as he slid onto an old love seat. Several women had transformed the seat by stripping away the decomposing leather and replacing it with a soft fabric that made it look almost new. He was so tired at this point, he would have sank down onto a mound of hay.

Struggling to keep his eyes open, he still needed an answer to the question that had been nagging him since the first Jeep-load of people had arrived at the would-be medical clinic's front door.

He'd whispered his question so quietly that the few people who were still in the house, either packing up their tools or carrying out the last of the debris, hadn't even heard him speak.

Tina was among the remaining few. Tired herself and having put in a really long day that had begun at four that morning, she knew no one would have faulted her for passing on this fast-paced building renewal the others had engaged in. But she had her own reasons for participating. A recipient of the kindness that Forever dispensed so easily, she thought it was only right to pass on a little of the same to another newcomer.

Looking the doctor's way now, she debated whether or not she'd actually heard his voice or just imagined it in her exhaustion.

She drew closer to him and asked, "Why what?" She sank down next to Dan on the sofa.

For just a moment, her closeness made him forget about everything else. Some women lost their appeal close up, because all their flaws were magnified. Others only became more appealing the closer they came. Tina fell into the latter category. It took several beats for him to remember what he was asking.

"Why did all of you go out of your way like this and do all this work?" He just didn't understand why anyone would work so hard to improve things for a stranger.

The house was far from perfect, but it was in much better condition now than it had been eight hours ago. Not only that, but several of the men had left, promising to be back tomorrow to complete their projects.

When the good citizens of Forever got rolling, it was a little like being in the path of the forces of nature. "Because that's what they do," she told him simply.

Tina paused, thinking back to how she'd felt when she'd first passed through the town. She'd been utterly isolated and alone, despite the fact that she was with Don and had Bobby with her. Despite the fact that she knew Olivia was out there somewhere, most likely looking for her. At the time, Forever had seemed like just another small town to pass through. A small town to look down on if she noticed it at all.

She knew better now.

"People in Forever see something that needs doing and they do it." She smiled fondly, once again thinking how lucky she'd been to find this place. "They look out for one another."

Apparently, Dan thought. But it still didn't make sense to him. He liked things to be logical, and lately, nothing was. If logic had existed, he would have been the one who'd died and Warren would have still been alive.

"But why?" he pressed. "What's in it for them?"

Tina shrugged. Some questions didn't come with explanations. She'd been in Forever for close to seven months now and not a day went by that she wasn't grateful for having passed through the town. Who knew where she'd be if it had been any other place.

"A good feeling, I guess." She saw the look that came over the doctor's face and speculated on his thoughts. "They didn't do it to trade for favors, or to make you feel indebted to them. In this case, they did it because they're thrilled to finally have a doctor in the town and they just wanted to show you their appreciation." She glanced around at the surrounding area. "If this house had been in top shape instead of falling apart the way it was, you would have probably been inundated with pies and cakes and more homemade jam than you *ever* knew existed."

Tina laughed, thinking of some of the women she and Olivia had become friendly with. "You still might be. I'd gauge my calorie intake if I were you," she warned. "They make fantastic pies and cakes here."

"You keep saying 'they,'" he noted, curious about

the distinction. "You don't feel the same way the others do?" Even as he asked, it didn't seem congruent, given that she had joined in the work and was still here, even after so many of the others had already left.

"Actually, I do. Now," she qualified. She could see that she'd raised more questions for him than she'd answered. "Olivia and I haven't been here all that long, so I'm still getting used to the idea of being part of this town. And of the way they think."

Her accent was just as lilting as the other people in the town. "Where are you from?"

"Olivia and I grew up in Dallas," she told him. Looking back, it felt as if her childhood—and most of her life, really—belonged to another world. She'd never felt as relaxed, as happy, as she did once she'd settled in Forever.

Dan couldn't picture someone who'd lived most of their life in a sophisticated city like Dallas willingly moving to a postage-size town that seemed almost rural in comparison.

"What brought you here?"

Tina sat up a little straighter. "Circumstances," she said evasively.

And that, he thought, was all he would get out of her on the subject. At least for now. Well, he could respect that. After all, he wasn't about to talk about why he was really here, either. He'd told the diner owner that he was here to take his brother's place, but he hadn't elaborated on the circumstances, or the oppressive guilt he felt. The guilt that popped up at any given time, delivering a sucker punch to his gut when he was least prepared for it.

Glancing down at her hand, he noted the absence of a wedding ring again. And, he had to admit, his curiosity chafed at him. Again.

But that was a question for another day, he decided. Right now, most likely, if she was inclined to tell him he'd probably fall asleep in the middle of her answer.

Turning her head, Tina noticed Rick approaching them. She and her brother-in-law made eye contact.

"Looks like my ride's ready to go," she told Dan. With one hand on the arm of the sofa, she pushed herself into an upright position.

Dan found he had to do the same in order to stand up. Eighteen-hour shifts notwithstanding, he couldn't remember *when* he'd ever felt so incredibly tired before. Every part of his body ached and a small voice in his head whispered a warning, *Wait until morning. This is nothing.*

"All set?" Rick asked as he joined them.

Tina nodded, then looked around. She'd expected someone else to be with him. "Where's Olivia?"

He nodded toward the front door. "In the car. Probably falling asleep," he guessed. For Dan's benefit, he explained his current problem with the woman who'd managed so effortlessly to capture his heart. "Olivia keeps trying to prove that she's still a superwoman, capable of juggling twelve things in the air even though she's more than eight months' pregnant. I tell her it's okay to slack off a little now, but she just won't listen."

Rick laughed, shaking his head. "I guess it's just hard to keep a good woman down."

"I think she'd like to hear that from you in person," Tina told him.

"That would only encourage her to do more. You know your sister."

Tina blew out a breath. The momentary second wind she'd gotten, talking to Dan, was gone. All she wanted to do was crawl into bed. She silently blessed Miss Joan, who she knew had put Bobby to bed long ago. The woman doted on the boy.

"You're probably right," she agreed. "But we've got a doctor in Forever now. He can take care of Olivia if she needs anything. You can stop worrying about my sister so much." Tina turned to the other man. "Right, Doctor?"

Dan preferred that his first challenge in this town would not involve a premature delivery.

"You keep right on keeping an eye on her," Dan advised. "Nothing ever takes the place of good common sense."

Rick laughed. "I'll tell her that. Nice to have someone agree with *me* for a change," he underscored, looking at Tina significantly.

"Hey, I'm always on your side," she reminded him with a grin that Dan, even in his tired state, found incredibly sexy and engaging.

"Yeah, right," Rick cracked, then looked at Dan one last time. "See you later, Doc."

The etiquette that his uncle had always held so dear would have dictated that he walked the sheriff and Tina at least to the door. But that was only if he had the actual energy to do so. Dan decided he needed to conserve what little he still had available in order to make his way up the narrow staircase to the second floor and the bedroom that waited for him.

"Thanks for all your help," Dan called out.

"Don't mention it," Rick answered.

The next moment, the door closed behind them and Dan suddenly realized that he was alone. Finally alone. It was the first time since he'd stopped his car to look down on the town that would be his home for the next nine months.

It felt good not to be surrounded by the hum of continuous voices.

For half a second, he debated just going to sleep right there on the love seat. But while it was all right to sit on, the thought of spending the night on the somewhat lumpy cushions was far from enticing.

He pointed himself toward the stairs.

The large box that one of the women had brought from Miss Joan sat open on a makeshift table someone else had dragged out into the reception area. Earlier, the box had been filled to overflowing with a variety of different sandwiches. To his surprise, there were still several left. Not that he could eat anything. Eating required chewing and he was much too tired to chew.

He'd have them for breakfast, Dan decided as he walked past the open box. Right now, the only thing he wanted to do was make it up to the bedroom and fall flat on his face onto the mattress.

This acutely reminded him of the marathon sessions

he and Warren had in at the hospital as interns and then as residents. Warren had thrived on them but he'd barely survived.

Thank God those days were behind him. The lure of getting a good night's sleep was just too tempting to pass up. It was one of the reasons why he'd picked radiology as his field. No one ever called a radiologist at three o'clock in the morning to take an emergency X-ray. They always found a way around it. Or ran the machine themselves.

Clutching the banister and pulling himself up one step at a time, Dan finally made it to the top of the landing. He hadn't realized until this moment that his knees had become unbelievably wobbly. So wobbly he had his doubts for a moment that they could support him. He let go of the banister very gingerly. When he remained standing, he felt like rejoicing.

There wasn't a part of his body that wasn't exhausted.

Stumbling into the slightly larger of the two bedrooms, Dan fell facedown onto the new mattress that had been brought in. He figured he'd be asleep in a matter of seconds. If Tina had been standing in front of him, dressed in nothing more than a smile, he wouldn't have been able to do anything about it.

His face pressed into the mattress, Dan's eyelids sprang open in total stunned surprise.

Where the hell had that thought come from?

He hadn't even been thinking about the woman just now. Yes, she was attractive, he'd already admitted as much, but that kind of thing didn't *really* matter to him right now. He was here for one reason and one reason only and that reason did not involve socializing with sexy blondes.

As exhaustion restaked its claim on him, Dan remembered that he'd forgotten to empty his pockets. He got as far as putting his right hand into his pocket.

Forever's new, temporary doctor was asleep before he could pull his hand out of his pocket again.

"Mama."

The tired, croaky, pleading voice penetrated Tina's dreamless sleep.

As a teenager, she'd been known to sleep through anything. Olivia used to tease her that she could sleep through the Apocalypse, not to mention any number of natural disasters or disturbances of nature, including, but not limited to, earthquakes, tornadoes and thunderstorms.

Back then it seemed like nothing could rouse her. Certainly not any man-made noise.

Motherhood had changed all that. These days, the slightest sound coming from the direction of her baby's crib had her sitting up, awake in an instant if not immediately alert.

Blinking, Tina tried now to pull herself together. "What is it, honey?" she called put soothingly, finding her way across the small guest room to where Rick and she had set up Bobby's crib in Miss Joan's house.

A full moon streamed its light in through the open window, illuminating her path.

Ordinarily, when her son called for her in the middle of the night, Bobby would be standing up in his crib, sometimes even bouncing in it, depending on whether he was hungry or thirsty—or if he needed to have his diaper changed.

But this time, mercifully, no pungent odor greeted her nose and Bobby was not the living embodiment of sheer charged energy the way he usually was. Instead, the towheaded toddler was lying down in his crib. This was definitely out of character for her son.

Tina blinked twice, trying to focus. She didn't want to turn on the light because she'd learned from experience that that would only wake him up and make him think it was morning. There was no containing him then.

She really needed to get some sleep and if Bobby wound up being fully awake, Tina knew that she hadn't a prayer of getting as much as a minute more of shut-eye from now until tomorrow night.

She was running on empty as it was.

For a moment, listening and not hearing his typical babble, Tina thought he'd gone back to sleep. But instead of tiptoeing away, she lingered a couple of beats longer. She had no idea what made her touch her son's forehead. Most likely some motherly instinct that had set in and become part of her makeup ever since the day her son was born.

As her fingers brushed against Bobby's forehead, he whimpered.

The heat she felt on his skin registered at the same time. Real concern took hold of her.

"Oh, honey, you're burning up," she cried. The fever seemed to have come out of nowhere.

Leaning over Bobby's crib, she bent over far enough

to resort to using what was considered to be every mother's true thermometer. She brushed her lips against her son's forehead.

It wasn't her imagination.

Bobby *was* burning up. He'd seemed a little listless when she'd seen him earlier, before going to help out at the doctor's place, but at the time Bobby's forehead had been cool.

That was the problem with babies. She'd read all about it in one of the half a dozen books she'd picked up on parenting a toddler. Children up to the age of seven had a tendency to run high fevers at what seemed like a moment's notice. They were just as likely to be fine within an hour's time but she wasn't about to be complacent and just wait it out.

She turned on the lamb-shaped lamp Miss Joan had given her and looked down at Bobby. His small face was flushed, his eyes looked liquid-y and as he whimpered again, his voice sounded scratchy to her.

He'd had his share of colds, but this was the first time that he'd felt so feverish. Tina took a deep breath. She told herself not to panic, but it wasn't a piece of self-advice she was about to take.

She needed to do something to get Bobby's fever down, but she'd just read an article in the paper about the uncertainty of feeding even a baby aspirin to a child as young as he was.

Indecision hovered over her as Bobby began to cry. Tina could feel her panic heightening.

Just then, she heard a knock on her door.

"Everything all right in there, Tina?" Miss Joan's voice came in through the door.

No, no it wasn't.

The next moment, Tina was pulling open the door, grateful to have someone to turn to. "Bobby's burning up," she cried.

Miss Joan hurried into the room, her ankle-length pink robe flying open on either side of her. She quickly assessed the situation herself with one brush of her fingertips against the toddler's sweaty forehead. "Throw something on and wrap him up in a blanket," Miss Joan instructed. "It looks like Dr. Davenport is about to have his first Forever middle-of-the-night emergency call."

Tina had just been thinking the same thing, but hearing the words said out loud made her hesitate for a moment. She didn't want to come across like one of those hysterical mothers.

"You don't think I'm overreacting?"

Kind hazel eyes met hers. "I'd really be worried about you if you weren't." Miss Joan gave her hand a squeeze. "Just remember, it's better to overreact and be sorry than to ignore the problem and run the risk of being even sorrier," the older woman told her. "Just give me a second to throw something on so I'm decent," she told Tina.

She began to hurry out of the guest room and back to her own, but then Miss Joan paused. She lightly touched Tina's face, cupping her hand against her cheek. "Don't worry, honey. Everything's going to be all right. Babies are very resilient."

Tina only wished that she could be.

Giving her a quick, reassuring smile, Miss Joan

hurried from the bedroom to her own. For a second, Tina remained frozen in place, struggling not to allow fear to get the better of her.

The next moment, she snapped out of it and flew to the closet. She quickly pulled on a pair of jeans and a sweater. She didn't bother putting on either a bra or underwear. All she was focused on was Bobby.

"Don't cry, Bobby, don't cry," she said over and over again, trying to soothe her son. "Dr. Dan'll make you all better." She said the words for both their benefits.

Tina sincerely prayed that she was right.

Chapter Six

Dan was completely dead to the world, sleeping the sleep of the severely exhausted, when the sound of urgent pounding woke him.

Prying open his eyes, at first he thought it was just part of his dream. A throbbing headache in the making, or something along those lines. It took him more than a minute to realize that the pounding existed outside his imagination.

When he finally did wake up, Dan was completely disoriented. So much so that he didn't know what day of the week it was or even, for that matter, *where* he was. Nothing looked familiar.

Like an array of items raining down on him from a collapsed overhead shelf, awareness took hold and startled thoughts pelted him.

He remembered.

Everything.

The good and the bad.

He was in a house in the middle of a hopelessly rural area. His home for the next nine months unless some miracle absolved him of guilt and provided a doctor for the town at the same time.

The pounding was still going on.

Dan pulled himself up into a sitting position, trying to get his bearings and focus. It wasn't easy. He felt as if he'd just risen from the dead or, at the very least, woken up from a coma. He dragged his hand through his hair, trying to think.

What the hell was making all that racket? The pounding wasn't stopping. If anything, it got more urgent and it came from downstairs, at his front door.

Some kind of an animal? A grizzly?

The thought brought a chill down his spine. Promise or no promise, maybe coming out here in Warren's place wasn't such a good idea.

Above the pounding he thought he heard someone calling his name. Okay, not a grizzly. Grizzlies didn't actually knock, and talking bears only existed in cartoons.

The relief that it wasn't an animal was short-lived. Damn it, someone wanted to see him? Now? This was the middle of the night. Didn't these people sleep?

Swallowing a few choice words, Dan reached for his jeans only to realize that he still had them on. He'd never taken them off when he fell into bed. He'd just been too tired.

If possible, the pounding became louder and even more urgent.

"I'm coming, I'm coming," he called out, even though he knew that more than likely, his voice wouldn't carry all the way down the stairs and out to the front door.

This had better be an emergency, Dan thought, feeling equal parts groggy and angry at the same time.

Clutching the banister to keep from pitching forward as he made his way down, he still hadn't managed to pull himself together by the time he got to the bottom of the stairs.

Unfamiliar with where the light switches were located, Dan half stumbled, half groped his way to the front door. When he walked into a table, more choice words popped up in his head as pain radiated up and down his shin until it felt as if it had reached the very roots of the hair on his head.

"What?" he shouted as he yanked open the door.

The next instant, when he saw Tina on his doorstep, holding a little boy against her, all the anger drained out of him. She looked completely distraught.

It was Miss Joan who spoke, answering the tersely voiced question as she ushered Tina and her son across the threshold, elbowing him out of the way and forcing him to step back.

The moonlight illuminated them. The older woman appeared exceedingly tense. "The baby's running a high fever. He had a fit in the car."

"A fit?" Dan repeated. And then he realized what she had to be trying to tell him. "You mean he had a convulsion?"

Pressing her lips together to keep a sob back, Tina nodded her head. Seeing Bobby like that had frightened her half to death. One moment she was in the backseat, holding Bobby to her, rocking slightly and trying to reassure him with soothing words, the next, she felt him stiffen in her arms and begin to jerk spasmodically no matter how hard she held on to him. It was a struggle to hang on to him. She had no idea what was happening to her baby.

All the years in medical school and at the hospital came to the foreground and took over. He wasn't groggy anymore.

"Bring your son into the exam room," Dan instructed as he lead the way.

This time, he managed to locate the light switch on the wall. It didn't occur to him until later to question why there was power running through the wires. After all, the house had stood empty all this time. Days later, he discovered that once Warren had answered Miss Joan's letter requesting for a physician to come to Forever, the woman had had the electricity, gas and phone all turned on so that there would be a minimum of inconvenience to deal with when the doctor came to open up his practice.

Tina lay Bobby down on the exam table. She and Rick's sister, Mona, had cleaned this room earlier, little did she realize that she would be back here within hours and that Bobby would wind up being the doctor's first patient.

The knots in her stomach tightened even harder as she watched the new doctor peel back Bobby's pajamas and examine him.

Bobby cried pitifully throughout the entire checkup. His cries turned into a shriek of protest when Dan attempted to insert a rectal thermometer into its targeted area in order to take his temperature.

"Hold him down," Dan ordered Tina sternly.

"I'm trying," Tina cried, frustrated.

Observing, Miss Joan felt she knew the makings of a disaster when she saw it. "You think that's wise, doing it that way, Doc?"

He knew what the woman was saying. If the little boy moved around too much or made any sudden moves, there was the very real risk of snapping the thermometer. If a piece of it lodged itself in the boy's rectum, extraction would be difficult.

"Probably not," he conceded, stopping. "But that still remains the most accurate way to get a reading of a child's temperature."

"My guess is a ballpark figure would do. Bobby's burning up," Miss Joan said.

Yes, he was, Dan thought. Setting the thermometer aside, he had Tina turned the boy over on his back. With quick, efficient fingers, Dan quickly examined the boy's small, lean body. There was no sign of a rash or any skin eruptions.

"Has he had his shots?" he asked Tina, then elaborated in case she wasn't following him. "You know, MMR. For measles, mumps and rubella. Also the one for whooping cough?"

Tina nodded in response to each injection. She'd been very diligent about that, seeing that Bobby received all of his immunizations. She even kept a log as to when each had been given to him.

"Good." The boy was still crying and looked utterly miserable, as well as flushed. "Is he allergic to any medication?"

She wanted to urge the doctor on, to make him do something to make her son better, not sit here and play twenty questions. But she knew Dan was just doing his best. She shook her head. "Not that I know of."

Nodding as he took the information in, Dan knew what his next course of action would be. "Stay with your son. I'll be right back."

Leaving the exam room, Dan hurried to the tiny room that was to act as his office. He'd locked up the medical bag he'd brought with him from New York, placing it into the only closet that appeared to have a working lock. Opening the closet now, he took out the stereotypical black bag and rummaged through it until he found what he needed.

Moving quickly, he returned to the exam room.

"Is he going to be all right?" Tina asked, her voice cracking under the strain of emotions.

Taking a syringe, Dan drew the proper amount for what he needed. "Your son should be fine in a few hours," he assured her, raising his voice to be heard above the pitiful crying.

Tina didn't take her eyes off the syringe in his hands. "What's that?"

"I'm going to give him a shot," he said needlessly. "Tylenol," he added. "To bring his fever down."

There weren't many over-the-counter medicines in her medicine cabinet, but she was familiar with this one. Or so she thought. "Doesn't that usually come in a pill bottle?"

"This is a much bigger dosage," he told her. "And it's a lot faster. It'll go directly into his bloodstream. It's the fastest way to start getting his fever down." He took a breath as he looked down at the toddler who seemed to be all arms and legs. "Now this is going to sting him and I need him to remain very still so you'll have to hold on to Bobby very tightly." There wasn't a trace of humor in his face as he asked, "Think you can do that?"

Tina nodded vigorously. Gathering the boy to her, she pressed the child to her chest. "I can hold him steady," she assured him.

His eyes met hers for a moment. "Good." Tina felt as if he was infusing her with his strength.

Very carefully, Dan inserted the needle into the fatty portion of the boy's thigh. Bobby's screams intensified, but Dan didn't allow it to distract him.

Finished, he removed the needle quickly and stepped back, inserting that part of the syringe into a hazardous waste disposal container that he'd packed along with his bag for just such an occasion.

Finally, utterly exhausted, Bobby's cries transformed into whimpers, which in turn hitched and became hic-cups. Before long, the boy finally fell into an uneasy silence. Within moments, drained, Tina's son curled up in her arms and went to sleep.

Only then did Tina let out a ragged breath. "I don't know how to thank you," she began, amazed at the re-markable difference in her son. Her ears were still ring-ing from Bobby's cries even though he wasn't crying anymore.

"It's not over yet," Dan warned her. He saw appre-hension come into her eyes. "I'd like to watch him for at least the next half hour to make sure that he doesn't relapse."

She wasn't planning on getting any sleep tonight anyway so she was more than prepared to monitor Bobby. "I don't want to put you out any more than I already have."

Silent for the past few minutes, Miss Joan spoke up. "Man's a doctor, Tina. This is what he does. Let him do his job." She flashed a smile at Dan. "I'll make us some coffee."

When last he looked, there'd been nothing in the pantry. He didn't even have a clue where the grocery store was. He'd planned on making a pit stop at the woman's diner in the morning for some breakfast, leaving the last two sandwiches for his lunch.

"I don't have any coffee," he told Miss Joan.

"Didn't say I was going to make *your* coffee, now did I?" Miss Joan responded with a laugh. With that, she left the room.

There was no doubt about it, this was a very unique group of people. "She's not going to pass her hand over a cup of water and turn it into coffee, is she?" Dan asked Tina. He was only half kidding.

Normally, the very idea was laughable, but there was something a little unnerving about the diner owner. He had the feeling that "Miss Joan" couldn't be rationally explained.

As far as Tina was concerned, the doctor had just given her back her son. Tina took pity on him and de-mystified the older woman. "Miss Joan usually has things in the trunk of her car for 'emergencies' such as this," Tina told him. "Said that where she came from, she learned that she needed to always be prepared."

Wasn't that the mantra of the Boy Scouts? "Where did she come from?"

Tina shook her head. "Nobody really knows for sure," she admitted.

That didn't make any sense to him. Didn't these people have any curiosity? "And nobody ever asked her about it?"

"They did, but supposedly she always changed the subject." Tina shrugged ever so slightly, taking care not to disturb the sleeping cherub in her arms. "They figure if she wants to keep it a secret, it's her right. They weren't going to pry."

Dan supposed that the young mother had a point, although his curiosity had been aroused.

For now, he let the subject go. "How does he feel?" he asked, nodding at the boy in her arms.

Ever so lightly, she kissed Bobby's forehead. Her face dissolved into a wreath of smiles as relief flooded through her veins. "Cooler," she answered him. "See for yourself," she offered, straightening so that the sleeping boy was more accessible to him.

Dan touched the boy's forehead. In doing so, he also inadvertently brushed the back of his hand against the swell of Tina's breasts. He immediately pulled his hand away, but for all intents and purposes, the "damage" had been done. Contact had registered and they were both very much aware of it.

If he'd had any doubt—or hope—that she hadn't re-alized what had just happened, Tina's sharp intake of breath told him that she was utterly aware that the back of his hand had touched an intimately sensitive part of her body.

"Sorry," he apologized in a hushed voice.

"Nothing to apologize for," she responded in the same low tone. She lifted one shoulder in a deliberately careless shrug. "Wasn't your fault. I should have held him out to you a little better."

He appreciated the fact that she'd absolved him of any blame.

Trouble was, he wasn't sorry. Not deep down where it counted. Oh, he hadn't wanted to cause her any discomfort or embarrassment, but at the same time, the unintentional intimate contact had stirred something within him. Whispered to him that he was still alive, still able to react to outside stimuli.

But, by the same token, feeling that way fed his guilt. Here Tina was, half out of her mind with worry about her convulsing infant and what he'd done, intentionally or not, was tantamount to copping a feel.

There had to be a very special seat in hell reserved just for him, Dan thought as yet another salvo of guilt ambushed him.

He had no idea why he was even reacting this way. After all, at thirty-two, he wasn't some kind of wet-behind-the-ears sheltered novice when it came to women. The exact opposite was true. Ever since Rachel Carrow had seduced him when he was fifteen and she a worldly woman of seventeen, he'd enjoyed the company of beautiful, willing women.

So why did accidentally touching this one set off

alarms in his head and make it feel as if he'd singed the back of his hand?

It didn't make any sense.

Trying to pull his very scattered thoughts together, Dan managed to say, "You're right." When she looked at him sharply, he realized that she probably thought he was agreeing with the very last thing she'd said, that touching her hadn't been his fault. He spoke quickly to clear up the misunderstanding.

"Bobby's fever does seem to be going down. I would have thought it would take at least thirty minutes, if not longer. I've never seen anyone react to Tylenol that quickly before."

"I don't care why or how," Tina confessed. "I'm just glad that he's not burning up anymore." She tried not to think about how scared she'd been. All that mattered was that Bobby was going to be all right. "Doc, about the convulsion—"

"That was because of the very high fever. It happens a lot more frequently with small children than you think. But the shot will keep the fever down to a manageable level until it's gone."

She closed her eyes, savoring his words. "Thank God." Opening them again, she said, "Before I forget, how much do I owe you?"

He was not up to talking about money right now. He'd never been involved in anything as mundane as rates and fees and right now, had no idea where to begin or what was reasonable and customary around this area.

Dan shrugged. "Beats me. I haven't had time to come up with any rates yet." He had intended to leave billing to the office manager. But that obviously was not the setup around here. This lone-town-doctor role that he'd had to assume was a whole different ball game. "Let's just say it's on the house," Dan told her.

That smacked of charity, Tina thought, and she didn't need charity. But arguing about that now didn't seem right, either.

She hit on a solution. One professional good deed traded for another. "How about, once you're set up, I'll get your accounts in order?" He looked at her, a shade of confusion in his eyes. They were pretty eyes, she thought. As big and blue as Bobby's were. She could feel herself being easily spellbound by them if she wasn't careful. "I'm an accountant," she told him. "Or at least, I will be once I pass my last class."

If he couldn't have an office manager, he supposed that an accountant was the next best thing. "I might take you up on that," he replied.

She'd taken up more than enough of his time. Not to mention that he'd earned her undying thanks and loyalty, helping Bobby tonight. Holding the boy against her, she rose to her feet.

"Well, you're probably dead on your feet," she speculated. "Bobby and I'll just go—"

He put a hand on her shoulder, gently pushing her back down into her seat. "No need to leave just yet. I'm still monitoring him, remember? Besides, we've got coffee coming. Might as well drink it. I've got a feeling that Miss Joan doesn't take well to having people pass up her coffee after she's gone through all the trouble of making it."

Tina smiled, relaxing a bit. "You're a pretty good judge of character," she acknowledged.

No, he wasn't. But he had a feeling that he would have to learn how to be. A place like Forever required it.

Chapter Seven

After Miss Joan took Tina and Bobby back home, Dan thought he would get some much needed sleep and even possibly sleep in the following morning. He was mistaken.

It didn't exactly come as a total surprise. Because even as he lay down, he had the unsettling feeling that he was on borrowed time.

And he was.

Approximately two and a half hours after he'd fallen back asleep, it happened. Someone knocked on his door. Again. At first it was lightly, then with a little more force. It was by no means the kind of pounding that the door had been subjected to when Tina and company had appeared earlier, but just as persistent.

Added to that was the fact that the sleep he'd fallen into, despite his exhaustion, was not nearly as deep this time as it had been initially. Consequently he became aware of the knocking quite possibly even at the moment it began. And lastly, the knocking was accompanied by daylight, the appearance of which officially declared that any hope of getting more sleep was utterly futile.

Still dressed in the same shirt and jeans he'd been wearing for the past twenty-four hours, Dan promised himself a quick shower and change of clothing as soon as he saw to the person at the door.

He assumed it was Tina, back to report on her son's condition. Hopefully the boy was improving, Dan thought, hence the reason she wasn't pounding on the door but just knocking.

After pausing to throw some water in his face, Dan padded down the stairs, realizing belatedly that he'd left his shoes standing beside his bed. He'd get them when he went back to change.

He arrived at the front door, took a breath to help him focus better and turned the doorknob.

The greeting he was about to utter froze on his lips the moment he'd opened the door. Tina, for whom the greeting was intended, was not standing on his doorstep. But it looked as if almost everyone else in Forever was. Or at least a very large portion. Had they come back to finish the work they'd started yesterday?

If so, they were undoubtedly standing at the back of the serpentine line that extended from the porch through the unkempt front yard, all the way down to the curb because he recognized no one up front.

Dan didn't bother craning his neck to see, but he had his suspicions that the line continued down the dusty block.

At the very front of the line was a heavyset, burly man who looked passingly familiar now that Dan had a chance to really focus on him.

"Um, Miss Joan said you were open for business, Doc.

That you've already seen your first patient so it was okay to come." He paused, waiting for either a confirmation or a denial.

Dan was forced to admit that Miss Joan was accurate in her second statement since he'd treated Tina's son. But before he could say that the clinic wasn't actually officially open yet—and that it wouldn't be for at least several hours—the burly man, who introduced himself as John Sullivan, proclaimed his relief the second he heard the doctor give him a tentative "yes."

"'Cause I've got this pain that's been eating away at my gut for mebbe two weeks now. Mebbe three," John confided, dropping his voice several decibels. "I don't have time to drive all the way over to Pine Ridge and kill half a day or more waiting on a sawbones to have a look-see. But with you being right here..." His voice trailed off but there was no reason for him to complete his statement. They both knew what he was driving at. John Sullivan wanted an appointment. Now. "Can you help me, Doc?" he asked hopefully.

"I can certainly try," Dan responded, surprising himself as his own words registered.

He'd been schooled to answer conservatively, to make no promises unless he was certain of the outcome. Better yet, to make no promises at all, just a few vague sounds that could be left to the patient to interpret. More than likely, he should have replied with some evasive phrase like "We'll see," and assessed the situation before anything vaguely resembling a positive answer was tendered to the patient.

But apparently, twenty-four hours in this place of few

traffic lights was enough to soften his resolve—and his brain.

Maybe there was something in the water, Dan silently guessed.

And so it began.

One by one, patient after patient marched through his unorganized office, stating his or her problem and waiting for the doctor from New York to fix it.

Since part of his disorganization meant he had no charts or files prepared, Dan was forced to take notes about each patient's complaint on the various scraps of paper he managed to unearth.

Because of that, with each and every stroke of the pencil he made, Dan sank further and further into a quagmire that deep in his heart he *knew* he hadn't a prayer of extricating himself from. At least, not without some major help.

Miracles, as far as he was concerned, had been pulled off the shelves. No major help would be coming his way, possibly ever.

BY ELEVEN DAN HAD TREATED approximately sixteen patients, had twice that number of pieces of paper scattered on his desk, all of which related to the various ailments that had paraded through the clinic—and was convinced that he was going down for the third time.

When he heard the tinkling sound that the front door bell made for the umpteenth time—whose bright idea was it to hang a bell on the front door, anyway?—he thought that he had been officially sentenced to reside in hell.

He hadn't come up for air once. His only "breaks" occurred when he stopped to wash his hands in between patients. The only good thing was that, so far, all the patients, miraculously, had left the clinic satisfied that they would be getting better from that moment forward.

He didn't need medicine, he thought cynically. All he needed was an endless supply of fairy dust since obviously the power of suggestion with these people was able to move mountains. Tell them they would be all right and they took the remark to heart, convinced that it would be so.

Of course, he mused, having patients who were running a spate of remarkably run-of-the-mill ailments didn't hurt matters, either.

Less than thirty seconds after the sound of the last annoying tinkling bell had emanated from the front door, Tina Blayne stuck her head into his office.

Surprised and pleased to see her face, Dan temporarily suspended what he was saying to Mrs. Allen about the red rash on her son's neck in order to acknowledge Tina's presence.

"Hi. Is everything all right with Bobby?" he asked, guessing the reason for her sudden invasion of an occupied exam room.

The wide, content grin on Tina's face went straight to his gut, knocking the air out of him for a moment. In another venue, it might have been referred to as a sucker punch. In any case, he was unprepared for it or its effect.

"Everything's perfect," Tina told him happily. "He's bouncing back as if he was never sick in the first place."

Currently, her sister, who'd taken the day off from her work, was watching the boy, which in turn allowed her to pop by the clinic. "But that's not why I'm here."

He'd always been naturally suspicious and now was no different. Had Tina come down with some kind of an ailment herself?

Before he could ask Tina exactly why she was here, she showed him.

"Miss Joan figured you'd probably be very busy this morning and might need this." "This" turned out to be a huge container of coffee and a foil covered dish. Both of which she placed on the desk in front of him. "Breakfast," she announced with a flair.

Mrs. Allen rose to her feet, picking up the prescription he'd just written for an antihistamine salve for her son's rash with one hand as she held on to her five-year-old's hand with the other.

"We'll let you eat in peace, Doctor. Thank you again so much!"

Dan could only nod in response. He did, however, make another note on yet another scrap of paper.

It took him a second to realize that Tina watched him closely. When he raised his eyes quizzically to hers, she had her own question for him. "Is that how you're keeping records?"

This was definitely not business as usual as far as he was concerned. Dan was accustomed to dictating his notes into a recorder which in turn would then be transcribed by someone the office manager would assign to the task.

"I thought I'd just jot some things down now and input

them into my laptop later." Once he remembered where it was packed, he added silently.

Coming closer to his desk, Tina turned one of the pieces of paper around and glanced down at it. She saw what amounted to several sets of wavy lines. Nothing on the paper remotely resembled words as she knew them.

Humor quirked her mouth when she looked up at him. "Boy, it really is true what they say about a doctor's handwriting." Her eyebrows drew together in a quizzical line. "Can you actually read any of this?"

"Sure," he answered defensively. But when he turned the paper around so he could look at it, he couldn't make out any of the words, either. Frowning, he was forced to admit, "Most of the time."

"Hey, Doc, are you ready to see me yet?" A red-headed, bearded man asked as he stuck his head in through the doorway.

Feeling somewhat protective of him, Tina took it upon herself to answer for the doctor.

"He's having breakfast right now, Howard. But he'll be with you in a minute." She thought for a second, then added, "Why don't you come back in, say, about five minutes?"

"Sure thing." He eyed Dan sheepishly. "Sorry to interrupt your meal, Doc," Howard apologized as he withdrew.

Dan glanced in Tina's direction and smiled his gratitude. "Thanks."

She waved a dismissive hand. "Don't mention it.

Wouldn't want you suddenly fainting from hunger on us," she told him.

With that, she slipped out of the office before he had a chance to protest. Dan turned his attention to the breakfast before him. He ate slowly, enjoying his first moments of solitude in more than four hours.

It was short-lived.

Five minutes to the second—that had been the deal—the door opened again. Howard was back, looking like an errant, overgrown choirboy as he cocked his head and asked, "Now okay, Doc?"

There was no sense stalling and putting off the inevitable. He was here to treat these people in Warren's name and they weren't about to go away until he did.

Dan beckoned for him to enter the office. "Now's fine."

Coming in, Howard thrust a file folder at him and took a seat facing him. "She said to give you this."

"She?" Dan repeated quizzically, taking the folder from the man. Who was he talking about and what did it have to do with this folder?

"Yeah. Tina," Howard replied. "She said you'd want to look at it first—before we talk about my, um, problem."

Now he was really curious. Opening the folder he found a single yellow sheet of paper—not a piece of paper but a whole sheet—inside. He skimmed it and found what was presumably a brief summary of his present patient's personal information as well as the complaint that had brought him to the clinic in the first place.

Scanning the neatly written information quickly, Dan set the folder down on the side of his desk.

"She was right," he acknowledged. "I did need to see that first. Okay, Howard, let's go to the exam room and get started," Dan said. Getting up, he led the way out of the office. "So how long have you noticed this 'squeezing feeling' in your lungs," he asked, using the exact words that were written down in the folder.

"About a month or maybe a little bit longer," Howard said after a moment's reflection.

As they walked into the exam room, Dan glanced over his shoulder toward the reception area. He tried to get a handle on just how many more people waited to see him.

To his surprise, Tina was now sitting at the scarred desk he'd briefly debated sleeping on last night. Oblivious to being observed, she was busy taking information from another one of the people in the room.

To his dismay, he noted, albeit belatedly, that it was still standing room only within the reception area. He would be here all afternoon. Maybe even part of the night.

Resigned, Dan closed the exam room door behind him and got to work.

SOMEWHERE AROUND THREE O'CLOCK or so, he'd stopped glancing at his watch. There didn't seem to be any point. Eventually, he completely lost all track of time. One by one, on occasion by two, the patients just kept on coming, bringing him everything from colds, to indigestion, to what sounded like colitis, to simple requests for dieting instructions.

The latter had come from a severely obese sixteen-year-old boy who'd cut school to come see him without his mother's knowledge.

"She keeps calling it baby fat, Doc," the boy, Chad Barth, lamented. "And says I'll outgrow it. How can I outgrow it if she keeps putting these heaping plates of food in front of me?" he asked. To him, the dilemma he found himself in was serious. "And if I don't eat whatever she puts in front of me, she cries and tells me I don't appreciate how much she slaves over the meals so that I would grow up strong. Look at me, Doc," Chad groaned, a look of disgust and loathing entering his expression as he gestured at his wide body. "How much 'stronger' am I supposed to grow?"

This, Dan remembered thinking, needed a psychiatrist's input far more than it needed his. But, per force, he did what he could for Chad, outlining a general diet designed to make the strapping teenager leaner and, by that very fact, healthier—as long as he stuck to it. At least for the most part.

His voice quivering with emotion, Chad left the office, promising to stick to the diet or die.

Dan didn't remember that much drama being in his life when he was sixteen, but by then, there had been no doting mother, no father to look to as a role model. There was just himself to lean on and Uncle Jason to turn to for the finer creature comforts since it was Jason who was left to be the executor of his late parents' will.

He'd been almost rail-thin at the time, with the family doctor after him to gain weight, not lose it.

He closed Chad's file and silently wished the boy well.

Dan soon realized he'd been alone in the room for almost three minutes without having someone peer in to ask if he was ready for him or her. It was a little after six. Afraid to hope that the endless stream of patients had finally stopped flowing, he got up from his chair and slowly went out into the reception area. Tina was still there, sitting at the desk just as he had seen her sitting several hours ago. She hardly seemed to have budged.

More surprising was that no one else was in the room *but* her.

Was the onslaught of patients *really* over? It seemed too much to hope for.

But he had to ask. "That it?" Dan deliberately looked at Tina, waiting for her to turn around.

He'd asked the question in such a low voice, at first Tina thought she'd imagined it. Turning around, she saw the doctor standing in the doorway. Poor man looked as exhausted as he had when she and the others had left last night. She felt guilty for being part of the reason he resembled thirty miles of bad road. A sexy road, but nonetheless a bad road.

"That's it," she confirmed, gesturing around the empty office.

"There's nobody else?" Dan pressed. "No wayward squirrel complaining of an acorn addiction?"

She laughed at the question. Dan found the sound strangely melodic—and enticing.

"Not that I know of, Doc."

He glanced at his watch and had trouble reading it. His eyes felt almost blurry. "What time is it?" he asked.

"Time to close up and get some dinner," Tina answered. She gathered the folders together and neatly piled them up. They needed to be alphabetized, but that could wait until morning.

It occurred to him that he was staring at her. "You've been here the whole time?"

She wasn't sure what he meant by "whole time." She could only attest to the time she'd seen on her watch when she'd walked in. "I've been here since eleven, yes," she acknowledged.

"Why?" Not that he wasn't grateful, but he had to know her reasoning.

Tina shrugged. "You looked like you were drowning. I thought you might need a little help. So I helped," she concluded.

Dan picked up a folder. He turned it around, examining it from both sides as if he was waiting for the folder to start talking.

Holding the folder up for her perusal, he asked, "Where did you get these from?"

"The trunk of my car," she told him cheerfully. "I'd just picked up a bunch at the general store. That and a pack of yellow legal pads." Both of which she used in her own line of work. It seemed to her that she could never get enough of either. "By the way, you're going to need to open an account at the bank."

The remark came out of left field. He had no idea

where it had come from or even why she was suddenly focusing on his personal finances. Granted, she would have no way of knowing, but he only intended to be here a matter of months, nine at the most. He didn't foresee the need for an account here. Anything he needed to do could be handled via his accounts in New York.

"Why?" he asked.

"Well, so you can deposit this," she told him simply, opening the center drawer of the desk. "Unless, of course, you'd rather just stuff this under your mattress," she added with a grin.

The drawer she'd opened for his perusal was stuffed to overflowing with money.

Chapter Eight

The whole scene seemed almost surreal to Dan. He stared as Tina opened the drawer all the way. "What is that?"

She looked up at him quizzically. "Money."

"Yes, I realize that, but what's it doing in the drawer?" Dan couldn't believe that the clinic's last occupant would have left behind an entire drawer full of money like that.

As he drew closer, he realized that the last occupant *couldn't* have left the money behind because most of the bills had color to them. Money printed using colored inks had only been in circulation in the past decade, not thirty years ago.

Had someone been using the uninhabited building to stash stolen money? It sounded far-fetched but he couldn't think of any other explanation for that much money to be there.

Tina looked down at the drawer and pretended to regard the various denominations.

"Lying down mostly," she replied to his question. And then, thinking she'd teased him enough, Tina gave him the real explanation. "From what little I know, most professionals, especially, rumor has it, doctors," she said with an amused smile, "aren't very efficient when it comes to charging for their services. So—I hope you don't mind," she qualified, "but I set up a temporary scale of rates for you. I've got you charging so much for a comprehensive exam—which since this was the first exam for everyone here, they all had comprehensive exams," she felt she needed to add, then continued. "So much for a follow-up visit, et cetera."

Tina placed the yellow sheet with the fees she'd thought fair to charge on the table and turned it so that the doctor was able to see for himself.

Dan looked at the numbers, trusting her to know what might be right for this area of the state. Right now, he hadn't a clue. What to charge for services rendered was not his field of expertise.

"When did you have time to come up with that?" he asked her.

"Since I've relocated to Forever, I've learned how to manage my time more efficiently. Besides, I hear it's something that all mothers know how to do. The mother's credo is Multitask or Die," she informed him with another engaging wide grin.

It was obvious to Dan that the petite, sexy blonde was very pleased with herself for collecting payment for his services. Beyond being surprised by all those bills stuffed into the drawer, seeing the money actually had very little effect on him. Money had always been part of his life. Neither he nor Warren had ever done without, at least, not without funds.

Indeed, they both could have used an emotional support system. Something they never received.

Dan knew that wasn't being fair to his uncle. Jason Davenport had done the best that he could. But, outside of a brother and a sister-in-law who'd died in a plane crash, abruptly leaving him to be the guardian of two young boys, Uncle Jason'd never had a family of his own. Confronted with this situation, the man had been completely out of his depth with no idea how to relate to anyone under the age of twenty-one.

So, what Uncle Jason, a die-hard playboy, lacked in experience he'd tried to make up for with money. He threw fistfuls of it at them. Consequently, he and Warren always had the best of everything.

The end result was that money, and the accumulation of it, had never meant that much to him. He was fairly certain that was not the case for the young woman who was now proudly displaying the bounty she'd collected for him.

Dan tried to remember just how many patients he'd seen today and drew a blank. He'd lost count early on in the day. Still, that looked like a great deal of money in that drawer.

A hint of skepticism entered his eyes as he asked, "You sure you didn't overcharge them?"

She was utterly sure. After all, her allegiance was to the people here, not to the man who was, for all intents and purposes, still a stranger.

"If anything, you were being generous with your time," she assured him. "And they *did* save both time and the money they'd be spending on gas, not having to go to Pine Ridge," she reminded him. "That's a savings in itself." She cocked her head, regarding him with curiosity. She tried to get a handle on him. Was he *really* that selfless? "Did you just think you were seeing them for free?"

"To be honest, I never thought about that part of it," Dan admitted.

This put him right up there with Doctors Without Borders and all the other various physicians who went into less than hospitable places to tend to the weak and the sick. He had just gone up several more notches in her estimation. "You, Doc, are a true humanitarian," Tina told him warmly.

Processing her declaration, he realized that she had to have misunderstood his meaning. But as he started to correct her, Dan decided against it. It was rather nice being regarded as someone who'd done something for another human being without any thought to his own gain.

Sort of like Warren.

God, he missed his brother.

Still, he really didn't want her making him out to be special. Dan shrugged in response to her compliment. "I just wanted to get to the last person in line, that's all."

She was not about to let him wiggle out of this. He was a good man and he deserved to be told. Deserved to know that someone else saw him for what he was.

"I hear all good doctors are like that." Changing the topic slightly to keep from embarrassing him further, Tina began taking the money out of the drawer. As she did so, she counted the various bills and stacked them.

"Since the bank's closed by now, I can bring this over to the sheriff's office and have my brother-in-law lock it up for safekeeping until morning. You can open an account then."

"The town has a bank?" he asked in surprise. When she'd mentioned opening a bank account, he'd thought she meant in another town. He hadn't noticed any large lending institutions when he'd driven through Forever on his way to the clinic yesterday.

Tina deliberately opened her eyes wide as she replied. "Uh-huh. It's this big, pink piggy bank in the town square." She struggled to keep a straight face. That lasted approximately thirty seconds. Failing, she started to laugh.

Her laugh was light, melodic, like sunbeams riding the spring breeze. He liked the sound. "Very funny."

She hadn't been able to resist the wry remark. "Sorry. In case you're wondering, I really do know where you're coming from." When he looked at her quizzically, she elaborated. "I didn't think that there was a place less backward than Forever when I first passed through here. But I learned pretty quickly that there were a lot more important things than being urban and sophisticated. All in all, I really wouldn't want Bobby to grow up anywhere else," Tina admitted.

Everyone in town doted on the boy and looked after him. She certainly didn't lack for babysitters when she needed them.

They'd have to tie him to a post to get him to stay here one second longer than he had to, Dan thought. But there was no point in arguing with her about the merits of big city life as opposed to some place where the town fathers—or mothers—rolled up the sidewalks at night. To each his own, he supposed.

Finally finished counting the money that had been taken in today, she looked up and told Dan the total sum that had been collected. His expression remained the same. She took a guess as to why.

"I know that probably doesn't seem like very much to you, given what people pay for a doctor's visit in New York, but out here, it's still a bit."

The truth of the matter was, he was feeling somewhat guilty about having this money. It wasn't as if he needed it, or had come here hoping to make his fortune. Granted, if he were working for the hospital in New York, he'd have no qualms about accepting a sizable paycheck, but that was different. He wasn't directly taking someone's hard-earned money and putting it into his own pocket.

"Why don't you take half of that?" Dan suddenly suggested.

Tina looked at him as if he'd taken leave of his senses. "Excuse me?"

"Take half," he repeated. "I mean, if you hadn't come by and gotten everything organized the way you did, I wouldn't have collected anything—and on top of that, I'd probably be hip-deep in scraps of paper." He paused for a second, debating the next words out of his mouth, then decided she'd probably already guessed as much. "I've never run my own office before."

The amused smile in her eyes filtered down to her lips, curving them. He caught himself watching her lips longer than he should have.

"I kind of picked up on that," she told him. "But I still can't take your money—"

He was not about to take no for an answer. "Consider it payment."

"I was considering it pay*back*," she corrected, referring to her services, not his money. "For seeing Bobby in the middle of the night. You didn't charge me for that," she reminded him, and explained further. "I don't like being indebted to someone."

That made two of them, Dan thought. In his opinion, she had come to his aid in the nick of time. "Neither do I."

Tina paused for a minute, studying him. "I guess we're at an impasse."

Dan blew out a breath, then nodded. "I guess we are. Would you like to try to resolve this over dinner?" he suggested.

Tina's blue eyes widened as she suddenly remembered. "Dinner."

"You know, food, something to drink. Served after four o'clock," he prompted when she'd all but gone into a tailspin at the mere suggestion of going out to dinner with him. Was that a good sign, or a bad one? Not that he wanted her to think that he meant anything by the invitation. She'd helped him out, he wanted to show his appreciation in a simple manner.

"No." Tina shook her head at his response.

"It's not served after four o'clock?" he asked, confused. Was this another quaint local custom, like pitching in and fixing up the clinic? He hadn't seen any signs of a potential nightlife when he'd passed through yesterday. Maybe everyone went to bed early out of boredom.

Tina only shook her head harder, negating his question. "No, I was supposed to bring you by the diner for dinner. Miss Joan told me to bring you over there the minute you got done."

Dinner did sound like a pretty good idea right now, given the fact that his stomach was complaining and the last thing he'd consumed had come from Miss Joan's diner aeons ago. But before pleasure, he wanted to talk business. He needed to resolve this so that there'd be nothing weighing down his mind.

"Look, I'm not sure how you managed to get time off to help me this way, but is there any chance I might be able to hire you away from your boss and get you to come to work the front desk for me full-time?" Dan asked. He didn't care what it would take. He'd gladly pay her out of his own pocket for the duration if she agreed to work for him.

When she didn't answer immediately, he tried a little flattery to move things along in the right direction. "Things went a lot more smoothly once you took over."

Tina smiled, both at the compliment and at the doctor's misconception. But then, how would he know? He hadn't been in town long enough for anyone to tell him anything. That made him her responsibility, she thought, amused by the notion. Something else she wasn't planning on letting him know about.

"I'm my own boss," she told him. "So, yes, I think there's a chance you could get me to come work for you."

She rose, putting the money into a large manila envelope whose glue had faded from the sealing flap. She folded it down anyway.

"Let's get this over to Rick," she said, holding the envelope slightly aloft. "And then we can go to Miss Joan's before she starts getting together a search party to come find us."

"Miss Joan a relative of yours?"

The woman was like a second mother to her. Miss Joan had literally insisted that she and Bobby come live with her until she felt ready to find a place of her own.

"You and Bobby bring sunshine into my life, Baby Girl," the older woman had told her more than once. And the woman refused to accept any money from her for rent, arguing that she "save it for a rainy day" instead.

"In a manner of speaking," Tina allowed, sliding the manila envelope into her oversize shoulder bag. "She's my guardian angel."

Dan rolled her words over in his head, trying to fathom the meaning behind the statement. Holding the front door open for Tina, he waited until she stepped out onto the porch. "Someday you're going to have to explain that to me."

"Someday I will," she agreed cheerfully. She saw him checking his pockets and frowning. "What's the matter?"

He nodded toward the door they'd just closed behind them. "I don't think I got the key for the house from the deputy."

"There probably isn't one. Most people don't lock their doors around here," she informed him. "They certainly didn't thirty years ago." She saw the look of disbelief in his eyes. "The most outrageous thing that happens in Forever is when Miss Irene sleepwalks through the middle of town in her nightgown, or drives around town—also asleep—without it." She smiled as he continued to stare at her, stunned. "We're not exactly a hotbed of crime waves around here."

Tina stopped for a moment, trying to remember what someone had told her. "The last burglary in Forever occurred when Patrick Fields stole the high school mascot—a miniature pony named Clyde—and hid it in his room. He got a lot worse from his mother than he did from the sheriff," she assured him.

Despite what she said about the town's lack of crime, he felt uneasy about leaving the house open that way. He supposed that it would do no harm, inasmuch as he'd found a way to lock the cabinet with all the medications he'd brought with him in it.

He didn't have much else of value here and if the medications were safe, he could reconcile himself to the rest of it.

He walked with her to his vehicle. After dinner, he could always bring her back to pick up her car. "What do you do around here for fun?" he asked Tina.

"You mean other than steal miniature ponies?" she asked, amused.

He laughed, letting her get a jab in. "Yeah, other than that."

"Count stars," she told him. When she saw him looking at her skeptically, she tried to convince him that she wasn't pulling his leg. "I'm serious. Big cities have a way of blotting out most of the stars," she told him. "There's a whole sky full of them out here on any clear night."

He didn't see how looking up at the sky could be constituted as fun.

Tina could almost read his thoughts. It amazed her how in tune she was with this man.

"You can make a whole evening of it," she said, trying to convince him. "Pack a picnic basket, drive into a field, throw a blanket on your car and just lie across the hood and lean back on the windshield, looking up." Tina called it by its official name. "Stargazing," she explained. "You should try it sometime."

Actually, it didn't sound half-bad, he decided. "I'll need a guide."

Was he asking her out in a roundabout fashion? The next moment, she told herself that she was letting her imagination get carried away. "I'll keep that in mind." Her smile dimpled her cheeks. "Hard to miss an open field and stars, though."

"Everything's better with company," he reminded her. Dan watched in fascination as her eyes crinkled.

"You have a point," she agreed.

He had more than that, Dan realized, as he recognized the faint stirrings he felt. It meant he wasn't as numb as he'd thought he was.

But having emotions made him feel disloyal to his brother's memory. He couldn't forget why he came to Forever and that sooner rather than later he would leave.

TRUE TO HER WORD, their first stop was the sheriff's office. Dan rounded the hood quickly and helped Tina out of the car, although she looked as if she'd do just fine without his aid.

Walking into the single-story building with her, Dan was surprised to be greeted by the deputies as if he'd always been a familiar face around Forever. It nudged at a warmth within him that he'd thought long since atrophied.

Rick crossed to him, shaking Dan's hand warmly even though it was less than twenty-four hours since he'd last seen him. "What can I do for Forever's newest citizen?" he asked.

Dan didn't bother correcting the lawman's misconception. They'd find out soon enough that he wasn't planning on remaining in the town. Still, he saw no point in a discussion at this point. Whenever a replacement turned up, then he'd tell these people that this was merely just a temporary stop for him.

For now, there was business to tend to. "Tina said you could lock this up for the night for me."

Rick raised a quizzical eyebrow. "And *this* would be?"

In response, Tina deposited the contents of the manila envelope onto his desk.

"This," she elaborated.

Rick stared at the pile of money. "You have a little thing going on the side, robbing banks?" he asked wryly.

"My office manager remembered to charge people for coming in," Dan explained before he realized that the sheriff was only kidding.

Rick laughed and clapped him on the back. "I'll take

care of it," Rick assured him, sweeping the cash back into the envelope. And then he stopped as a thought occurred to him. "You want a receipt?"

Dan shook his head. "No need. I trust you," he said as he left the office with Tina. He thought of something as they walked out onto the sidewalk. "If everyone's so honest around here, why do we even need to lock up the money until morning?"

"Well, there's such a thing as too much temptation," she told him. "Some of the people around here aren't as well off as others and they could really use a hand up to get by. But, for the most part, you're right. The money would be safe left in your drawer."

"Then why did we just bring it to your brother-in-law?"

"Mostly for your benefit," she said honestly. "I figured being from New York City and all, you wouldn't sleep right knowing there was all that money lying around downstairs, calling out to every burglar in a fifty-mile radius." She managed to state the whole thing without grinning, but it hadn't been easy.

"You're making fun of me," Dan accused genially.

Tina saw no point in denying it.

"I am," she agreed, "but only a little bit." She held up her thumb and index finger, keeping them less than an inch apart to show him just how little.

He liked the way humor lit up her eyes. Dan had more than a sneaking suspicion that nothing in the night sky, even in this rural place, could compete with it.

Chapter Nine

At approximately six-thirty in the evening, the diner was doing a brisk amount of business, but there were still a couple of empty booths to be had. Because this was her territory, Dan let the woman who had bailed him out today pick out a table.

As he followed behind Tina, he found his path littered with cheerful greetings sent his way. At first, he thought the hails were all directed at Tina, but when a senior citizen on a counter stool specifically used his name when he extending his greeting, Dan realized that the people in the diner were saying hello to him, as well.

The entire scenario made him think of a scene directly out of a popular classic sitcom where everyone was purported to "know your name," uttering a greeting the moment someone walked through the establishment's door. Behavior like that was foreign to him. One day here and everyone acted as if he'd been born and bred in the town.

The New Yorker in him found it suspect. But another, small part, the part that had been the man to whom

Warren had looked up to, had to admit that he was some-what warmed by the genial atmosphere.

The moment they sat down at the table, Miss Joan made a beeline for the booth to take their orders herself. Or rather, to take his order.

"I already know what you'll be having," she told Tina, making a quick note on the small, old-fashioned pad she kept in the pocket of her apron. "She has the same thing every night when she eats here," Miss Joan whispered to him in the spirit of sharing a confidence.

Dan looked at Tina, raising a curious eyebrow. Waiting to be enlightened.

"It's chicken salad on rye," Tina confessed. She lifted her slim shoulders in a half shrug, then let them fall again. "What can I say? I'm dull."

Dull, he thought, was not a word he'd use to describe her. If anything, she struck him as the exact opposite. There was something very stirring about her that he hadn't quite been able to put into words. Maybe it was better that way.

"Stable and dependable," Miss Joan was saying, erasing the word Tina had used to label herself. "Nothing wrong with that. Besides, I make a pretty mean chicken salad sandwich," she told Dan with pride.

"All right, then make that two," Dan said. Closing the menu, he surrendered it back to Miss Joan.

Tina glanced at her watch and frowned. "Maybe you'd better wrap mine up to go, Miss Joan." The latter looked at her in question. "I really should be getting back to look in on Bobby and take him home."

"Don't you worry about him. Bobby's doing just fine,"

Miss Joan assured her. "I just called your sister not fifteen minutes ago to check on him. He's back to his old self. Got so much energy he's wearing her out, Livy told me. So sit. Eat," the woman instructed in a no-nonsense voice that wasn't to be questioned or challenged. "Catch your breath. Bobby'll still be there when you finish your dinner."

"I'm not all that sure if Olivia will be," Tina commented. These days, it was all Olivia could do to drag herself through her day. With one more month of pregnancy to go, her sister was more than ready to have the baby now and get back to her old self.

"It's good practice for her," Miss Joan tossed over her shoulder as she started walking back to the counter. "Lets her know what she's going to be in for. She'll be a mama in less than a month," was the woman's parting comment.

Shaking her head, Tina laughed softly under her breath. "She keeps closer tabs on Olivia's pregnancy than Olivia does," she commented to Dan.

He found her smile to be warm, appreciative and completely captivating as she added, "I think Miss Joan's practically adopted all three of us."

Certainly sounded like that to him, he thought. Curiosity nudged at him, prompting him to ask, "Doesn't she have any family of her own?"

Tina thought for a moment, then shook her head. "I know she's buried a few husbands but I've never heard anything about her having any children, which is really a shame. She's so good with Bobby."

"It's easier being good with other people's kids. If

something doesn't go right, you're free to back away and give the kid back to his parents," he said.

"That's awfully cynical, Daniel," she observed.

This was the first time she'd used his name. He liked the sound when she said it. But his opinion on the matter didn't change.

"It's a cynical world, Tina," he countered.

"No, it's not," she contradicted stubbornly. "It's what you choose to make it."

Silent for a moment, Dan studied the woman sitting across from him. She really believed what she said. Outside of Warren, he hadn't thought they made selfless and optimistic people like that anymore. People who obviously focused on only the good in their fellow human beings.

Maybe there was something in the water, he thought, amusement tugging at the corners of his mouth.

Miss Joan came by to bring them both coffee and then returned a second time with the promised sandwiches. The latter, he discovered after a single bite, actually did turn out to be the best chicken salad he'd ever eaten. The woman hadn't exaggerated.

They chatted through the meal and he found Tina exceedingly easy to talk to. It was hard to believe that a couple of days ago, he hadn't even known that she existed.

Fortunately for him, the conversation was so effortless and engaging because he slowly became aware of the fact that, for all intents and purposes, he seemed to be on display in the diner.

Whenever he glanced around, he caught someone

blatantly watching him. A few did it so intently as to scrutinize his every move. Either that, or doing their damnedest to piece together what he was saying to Tina from across the room.

"Do people read lips around here?" he asked, leaning forward so that only Tina could hear him. He deliberately placed his hand so that it blocked a clear view of his mouth.

Which only seemed to draw her attention to it, Tina thought. He had a nice mouth. A generous one. She caught herself wondering what it felt like, having that mouth pressed against hers.

She forced herself to focus on his rather strange question instead. "Miss Joan does, but I don't know about anyone else," Tina replied. "Why?"

Again his eyes swept around the area. A few people made eye contact and actually waved at him. What was *that* about, he wondered. "Because they're watching us so intently, I thought maybe they were trying to read our lips."

Tina smiled indulgently. He didn't understand. But he would. Eventually.

"You're new here. People are trying to find out whatever they can about you. As the 'mystery' man, it's only natural that you'd be the object of curiosity. You've given them something to talk about." She could see he wasn't happy about being the center of attention. That meant he had no ego, which was nice. "Don't worry, they'll stop looking soon enough."

"Was it like that for you?" he asked, curious.

She didn't need to think. It hadn't been all that long

ago. "Pretty much. Actually worse," she amended. "You're the noble young doctor, here to cure whatever ails them and make them feel good. I, on the other hand, was the single mother whose boyfriend almost wound up killing her."

He stopped eating and stared at her, debating whether she was being melodramatic, pulling his leg or telling him the truth. When she didn't follow up with a grin, he had an uneasy feeling that it was the last choice. "Seriously?"

She nodded, the picture of solemnity. "Very seriously."

Funny, she hadn't talked about this at all since it happened, not even with Olivia. But something about the look in his eyes just made the floodgates open and the words began to pour out.

"I had an uneasy feeling that things weren't exactly right with him and I managed to talk Don into letting me leave our son on Rick's doorstep—I didn't even know he was the sheriff at the time. It was just a handy front stoop as we drove out of town.

"Bobby had been crying for most of the morning and had really gotten on Don's nerves—not that he was the patient type to begin with. Don kept threatening to 'shut Bobby up permanently' if he didn't stop crying, so it wasn't too hard to talk him into leaving Bobby behind."

Dan watched her incredulously. "And you just put him on a stranger's doorstep? Just like that?"

She didn't know if he was judging her or just trying to understand. "It was either that, or risking having something awful happen to him. I went with the better odds."

"Why didn't you just leave with Bobby?"

A humorless smile twisted her lips. "Don wouldn't have liked that," she told him in a flat voice. "I was desperately trying to keep him from going off around people. At that point, I honestly didn't know what he was capable of," Tina admitted.

She was young, beautiful, intelligent. It didn't make any sense from where he was sitting. "How did you get mixed up with him in the first place?" he asked.

There was an ironic glimmer to the smile that came to her lips. "Haven't you heard? Women have a tendency to fall in love with bad boys. I certainly did. And Don was a prime A example of a bad boy."

Dan wondered what she'd say if she knew that he'd had a reputation as being one of those bad boys she was talking about. One of the last women he'd seen as a resident had called him that, saying that was how she knew there was no holding on to him.

"Most bad boys don't turn out to be psychopaths," he pointed out to her. Had she been drawn to this Don person because she had a need to fix things? To heal people who were broken?

"No, they don't," Tina agreed. "But Don was. He was in a class all by himself. After I put Bobby on Rick's doorstep, Don couldn't wait to tear out of town. When I asked him where we were going, he got this strange look in his eyes and said we were seeing a friend of his just over the border.

"When he wouldn't tell me the guy's name, we got

into an argument and suddenly Don's stepping down hard on the gas, driving straight toward a tree. When I screamed for him to stop, he laughed and said it was too late. We were going out in a blaze of glory."

A shiver worked its way down her spine as she recalled the awful events of that day and the terror that had gone through her. She'd been positive she would die in the middle of nowhere, going eighty miles an hour with a man who'd become unhinged.

"I have no idea why he said that or what came over him," she admitted. "One minute, Don could be almost sweet, the next, completely deranged." She shrugged, pushing the entire haunting incident away as she took a deep, cleansing breath. "Anyway, the good thing to come out of that was that Olivia and I wound up living here instead of Dallas."

It was obvious that she'd skipped a few sections in her narrative. "Just how did you go from A to B?" he asked her. "From Dallas to here?" Dan added.

"Olivia was looking for me—Don and I and the baby were living with her in her apartment at the time. I didn't think she'd come looking for me because all we did was argue whenever she was around. I was pretty horrible to her at the time," she acknowledged. She still felt guilty about that. "Olivia raised me when our parents were killed so I guess I just rebelled against her because she was my mother figure."

Tina pressed her lips together. All that had happened right before Thanksgiving last year. She'd done a lot of growing up since then. She vowed she would spend the rest of her life trying to make it up to her sister for what she'd put her through.

"When we took off, I didn't know that Don had stolen some of her jewelry, but I found out pretty fast." And was horrified that he'd stolen from her sister. "At the time I was cynical enough to think that she came after him because of the jewelry. I know better now." Her mouth softened as she said, "Olivia came looking for us because she loved Bobby and me and because she knew that Don wasn't any good for either of us. When we were growing up, Olivia had an annoying habit of always being right." Tina sighed. "And this was no different. She was right about Don. Right about a lot of things. She told me I was better off without him and she was *so* right about that." Tina toyed with her napkin as she spoke, folding and unfolding it. "Looking back, it was like having a cancer cut out. Without Don bringing me down, the world suddenly became a lot brighter."

She seemed so down to earth. He tried to picture her driving around the country with an out-of-control boyfriend, and failed. He supposed that people could change, even drastically, given the right set of circumstances.

"Was it Olivia who decided you should live here?" he asked.

It wasn't exactly linear, Tina remembered with a smile. They'd both returned to Dallas first—and Livy discovered she was absolutely miserable that far away from the sheriff with the sexy smile.

"After Rick came and got her, yes. He came all the way up to Dallas and told her he was willing to change his life around to be with her." Affection entered her voice. "That was when my big sister decided that a man like that was too good to let get away. And, the truth of it was, Forever had impressed her even though she hadn't wanted to let it. It impressed both of us," she admitted. "This is a great place to raise a baby."

By that she was referring to her son, he gathered. "Bobby," he said out loud.

Tina nodded. "Bobby. And the baby that Livy's expecting."

Dan laughed shortly. "I get the feeling you're leaving things out again."

"Yes, but that's a story for another time." Placing the napkin on the table, she smoothed it out as if it might be used again. "Right now, I really do have to be getting back."

Her car was still parked by the clinic. "I'll take you to your car," he told her, the tone of his voice telling her that this wasn't up for debate.

Dan looked around for Miss Joan and spotted her at the far end of the counter. Despite the distance, she was apparently one of the people given to observing him— and Tina. Catching her eye, he raised his hand to draw her over to their table.

Miss Joan came at her own pace, giving each a warm, approving smile. He got the feeling that the woman was not above playing matchmaker when the spirit moved her. She was in for a surprise if she did. He wasn't about to remain here any longer than necessary and he definitely wouldn't make any commitments, no matter how attractive the woman was.

"You two need something else?" Miss Joan asked when she reached them.

"Just the bill, Miss Joan," Dan said, taking out his wallet. "Dinner was very enjoyable." He couldn't help glancing in Tina's direction as he said it.

Miss Joan frowned and pushed his hand back. "Put that away, Doc," she told him sternly. "Your money's no good here. This was on the house." She'd been the one who had written a plea for a doctor to come to Forever and she was determined to be the one instrumental in making the doctor stay. Feeding him was just one of the pieces of her plan.

Dan had grown up with money and one of the lessons he'd learned was that people with money generally wanted more of the same. He sincerely doubted that anyone in this town that all but reeked of the work ethic could be viewed as wealthy, or even mildly well-to-do.

"Refusing money isn't exactly good business sense, Miss Joan," he advised her tactfully.

The woman appeared unfazed. "Wasn't thinking of it as business," she replied. "More like giving a friend something to eat as a way of paying him back for tending to a little boy I'm very fond of."

Friend.

The word shimmered in his head. It was way too early for that kind of a label to be bandied about so cavalierly and applied, he thought—unless Miss Joan was talking about Tina.

He grasped at a straw. Maybe Miss Joan was just including him because he was here with Tina. But somehow, he doubted it. Still, he had a feeling that if he pressed the matter, he'd somehow be guilty of insulting the woman and he really didn't want to do that.

Especially when he saw the warning look in Tina's eyes as she turned her head in his direction. So he put his wallet back into his pocket and thanked Miss Joan for the meal and her hospitality.

"I'll see you tonight," Tina said to Miss Joan as she rose to her feet.

Hair the color of bright flame bobbed up and down with a measure of feeling before Miss Joan turned away and walked back to the counter.

"You're coming back here later?" he asked Tina, his curiosity mildly engaged.

Why would he ask that? "No."

But she'd just told Miss Joan she'd see her later. He didn't understand.

"Then why—" He let his voice trail off, deciding that perhaps he was prying too much into this woman's life. He needed to back off—for both their sakes. He didn't want her getting the wrong idea and thinking that he was interested in her in any other capacity than someone who could help him during his stay here.

"I live with Miss Joan," she explained as they walked toward his car.

A lush, warm darkness enveloped them, promising no relief from the hot day that had come earlier. He would have to see about getting an air-conditioning unit put in, Dan thought. The night ahead at the clinic promised to be a sticky one.

"After Olivia and Rick got married, I didn't think it was right for them to have a sister-in-law and her baby hanging around, intruding in their space. Rick said that he was all right with having me live with them, but I think he was just being nice. Newlyweds need their privacy," she added with a touch of humor. "Lucky for me, Miss Joan volunteered to let me stay with her. Said she was tired of just hearing the sound of her own voice at night.

"So far, she hasn't gotten tired of hearing mine. But even so, I am saving up to get a place of my own." She had no idea why it was so important to her that he know that, but it was. She didn't want him thinking that she was one of those women who just let life happen to her. She meant to be in charge of her destiny—hers and Bobby's—from now on.

Dan walked even slower, nodding at what she'd just said. He used it to his advantage. "You can save faster if you take me up on my offer to come work at the clinic," Dan reminded her.

She'd been considering it—and leaning toward saying yes. For the most part, the different small business owners who were currently her accounting clients could all be juggled from home. She could work on their books at night or in her spare time. Keeping their accounts in order really didn't require that much time from her, she thought. And who knew, this could be a good opportunity for her to advance herself.

Working with the handsome, sexy doctor—who appeared to be unaware of just what kind of signals he sent off—was a good move, maybe for more than one reason.

Placing her hand in his, she said, "Okay, Doc, you've got yourself a deal."

She intended for it to be nothing more than two people shaking hands, closing a deal the old-fashioned way. Instead, she felt she'd opened the floodgates for something else. Something that, down the line, she might not be able to exercise control over.

Overwhelmed by her thoughts, she pulled her hand away as if she'd touched fire.

Because maybe she had.

Chapter Ten

Graduating from a first tier medical school, Dan was fairly secure in the belief that he was a good doctor with more than a reasonable amount of learning to fall back on. As a resident, he'd not only survived, but done well in one of New York's top hospitals. The experience had made him overconfident.

Almost from the beginning, Dan found himself learning things here. Each day his ego was whittled down a little more.

Being a doctor in a small town like Forever wasn't the same as having a practice in one of the larger cities. In hospitals like the one where he and Warren had done their residency, there were a myriad of rules to follow, a hierarchy to always be mindful of. Here it was more comparable to being in an improvisational theater. He found himself flying by the seat of his pants and making things up as he went along. The by-product of that was experiencing a great deal of satisfaction whenever he was right.

As an intern and then a resident, he was never on his own. Securing basic medications and ordinary supplies were not his concern. His job was to apply the wealth of his knowledge to the situation and the patient's needs and then move to the next patient. On those occasions when a case baffled him, there were always other doctors, residents as well as specialists, to turn to and consult with.

Here he had no one. Not to consult with or even to tell him where he could obtain the basic things he needed to ply his craft.

Well, he amended, that wasn't strictly true. He had Tina, who, although not a medical professional on any level, seemed to be operating purely by common sense rather than experience. Tina was the one to point out that he needed more supplies and medications than he'd brought with him.

And she was the one who reminded him that should he be called upon to have a patient taken to the nearest hospital, a hospital located in Pine Ridge some fifty miles away, he needed to have been granted privileges at that hospital to begin with.

Which was why they were currently on this odyssey today. He'd put a closed sign on his front door and had left with Tina for Pine Ridge the minute she was ready to go. It hadn't occurred to him to leave without her.

Because she'd been verbally reviewing all the things they needed to pick up once in Pine Ridge, he heard himself asking her, "You studied medicine?"

She certainly sounded as if she had, at least in some capacity. After a couple of weeks in the woman's company for the eight-hour plus shifts he found himself putting in, Dan felt that nothing about Tina Blayne would surprise him. She seemed very capable no matter what she turned her hand to.

Tina smiled, leaning back in the passenger seat. They were technically on a short business trip, but this was the first time she had kicked back since she, Olivia and Bobby had moved to Forever and she was making the most of it. It wouldn't last long.

"Not really," she replied.

"Just what does that mean?" he asked.

"It means whatever knowledge I have, I picked up by being on the other side of it."

That only made things more obscure, he thought as he looked over at her. There were miles and miles of nothing before them so he felt rather confident taking his eyes off the road for a second.

With a careless, dismissive shrug, Tina gave him a quick summary. She had no intention of dwelling any longer on a past she was trying to forget.

"When I was in the car accident, the medical transport that came for me took me to the hospital in Pine Ridge. I got to watch the action up close and personal— when I was finally awake," she amended. It was only now, after the space of a good nine months that she was able to divorce herself from the situation and keep it at bay well enough not to allow it to affect her—at least, not so that anyone would really notice.

Unless they *really* knew her.

She'd been through a near-death experience—and survived. That kind of thing changed a person, lingering in the recesses of their mind, waiting for an unguarded moment in order to haunt them.

Questions gave birth to more questions. Usually, he wasn't the curious type. He chalked it up to boredom. "Were you unconscious for a long time?"

Tina nodded. "Almost a week, so they tell me." A sympathetic smile curved her mouth. "Drove poor Olivia almost over the edge. She'd put up with a lot from me. In her place, I doubt if I would have been that forgiving—or that patient. The point I'm getting at is that the doctors even in a relatively small place like Pine Ridge have their protocol to follow. You don't have those kinds of restrictions." As if reading his mind, she added, "You also don't have that kind of support system."

She had that right. Sparing her another lengthy glance, he smiled. "Then it's lucky I have you."

She had no idea why that simple sentence or the sentiment should warm her the way it did. But she could feel the heat traveling up and down her limbs and shimmying along her spine.

With a shrug, she murmured "We'll see," trying to deflect any further attention from herself before he noticed she was trying not to blush.

And barely succeeding.

Once they reached Pine Ridge's hospital, leaving Dan's sedan on the ground floor, they went to Human Resources. The department turned out to be hardly more than a small office dominated by a large computer and an even larger woman whose fingers seemed to fly across the keyboard with only slightly less speed than a brand-new Boeing 797.

The woman entered his name into the databank and promised to send him papers to sign once she was able to verify his background and a few other pertinent, important details. She also gave him a heads-up as to where to secure some much needed supplies. Dan was down to his last precious antibiotics and had only one syringe left.

As they made their way to the proper area on the ground floor, Tina and Dan crossed paths with a tall, gray-haired physician in a flowing lab coat. In a hurry, he abruptly stopped when he passed them and, for all intents and purposes, executed a double take.

"Tina?" the doctor asked uncertainly.

When she turned to look at the man, it took her less than a few seconds to place a name to the face and also to remember where she knew him from.

She'd never forget.

"Dr. Baker," she cried warmly, giving him a quick hug before stepping back. "Hi."

The man who had treated her when she'd been brought in by the hospital ambulance, broken, bleeding and in a coma, seemed pleased to see her.

"How are you?" He clasped her hand between both of his, his eyes sweeping over her as if to make sure that she had indeed made a complete and full recovery. "You look wonderful."

"Thanks to some exceptional doctoring," she acknowledged, "I *am* wonderful."

Tina was well aware that her recovery, as extensive as it was given the circumstances, was nothing short of a miracle. She'd both accepted it and reveled in it. The alternative was too dark even to contemplate.

Inherently modest, Dr. Baker was quick to share the

credit for an operation that had taken well over five hours.

"And a miracle or two." His destination temporarily placed on hold, the doctor paused just to digest the sight of her. "What are you doing here?" Dr. Baker asked her. "The last I heard, you and your sister were heading back to Dallas."

They had gone back. For all of two weeks. And then Olivia broke down and admitted that she missed the sheriff. Missed him with an unshakable passion. About to pack up to go down to Forever, they were surprised by a knock on their door—Rick was on the other side, ready to do what it took to make Olivia part of his life.

What it took was moving to Forever.

"We live in Forever now," Tina told the physician. "We both decided that there was a huge advantage to living in a place where everyone's not rushing right over you so much." Suddenly remembering she wasn't here alone, she inclined her head toward Dan. "We finally got a doctor of our own in Forever. This is Dr. Daniel Davenport."

"Baker," the other physician said, shaking Dan's hand with feeling. "Nice to meet you."

Before Dan could say anything, Tina interjected. "Dan's here applying for operating privileges at the hospital," she explained.

Baker appeared delighted by the news. "Excellent. We could always use another good surgeon. Anything I can do to help?" he offered.

The smile in Tina's eyes quickly reached her lips. "As a matter of fact—"

Which was how, after transferring Tina's verbal list onto paper and then stopping for a quick bite to eat at the cafeteria, Dan and Tina wound up with a trunkful of supplies.

Driving back, Dan noted that the woman sitting in the passenger seat was still grinning from ear to ear fifteen miles into their return trip.

"You're looking pretty happy with yourself," he observed, amused.

She was. Very. For perhaps the first time since she and Olivia had come here to live, she felt as if she was finally giving a little back to the town that had embraced her.

Her eyes danced as she asked cheerfully, "Shouldn't I be?"

She would get no argument from him. If not for her connection, they might still be trying to secure the supplies. Hospitals guarded their wares zealously, especially from outsiders which, technically, he still was. Being part of the staff for all of two hours didn't exactly place him in the realm of the inner circle.

"You've got every right," he agreed, then, after a beat, brought up another subject. "Baker looked pretty taken with you."

Tina waved away the remark. "He was just admiring his handiwork. He was the one who put me back together again after the accident. If it hadn't been for Dr. Baker, who knows what condition I might be in? Or if I would even be around."

She tossed the remark off without allowing herself to speculate. There was no point in going down that road. She was the first to acknowledge that she'd been lucky and she intended to make the most of her second chance. Make the most of it and also continue to pass on kindness whenever she could.

"If I didn't mention it before," Dan said, and he knew he was pretty remiss when it came to expressing gratitude, "I appreciate you coming with me today."

They were getting closer to Forever. He glanced to his left. The scene caught his attention as it registered. The sun was making a huge production out of setting, rendering the kind of breathtaking scene that few in the city knew they were missing out on unless they happen to be lucky enough to be out in the desert—or the country—at just the right moment.

And even then, this sunset was in a class by itself.

"No need to thank me." She brushed off his gratitude. "After all, you're the boss," she reminded him.

He doubted if she actually believed that. The woman was probably just humoring him, having been told that male egos need stroking. His didn't need stroking—but he did like her company. "You could have taken the day off," he pointed out.

A day off would have meant doing nothing. She shook her head. "Doesn't appeal to me. I like working, keeping busy." And then, out of the blue, she suddenly ordered, "Pull over."

"What?"

Tina repeated her instruction, this time with more urgency. "Pull over."

There wasn't much of a shoulder to the two-lane

highway, but he did as she asked, pulling over to the highway's right shoulder.

"What's wrong?" he asked.

The expression on her face was the last word in serenity. Wouldn't she have looked agitated if something was wrong?

The next moment, she reassured him. And explained.

"Nothing's wrong," Tina remarked calmly. Then, before he could demand to know why she had him pulling over if nothing was wrong, Tina pointed to the view to his left. "Look," she urged. "Isn't it beautiful?" she asked in almost a hushed whisper.

So he looked. And saw a round, crimson-gold ball sinking in the distant horizon. Slowly disappearing by inches as it prepared to pay a visit to another part of the world.

Dan also looked at the woman who pointed all this out to him. Her face was almost transfixed. As radiant as the sunset she was so intent on showing off. For his money, she was the wonder of nature to appreciate, not another sunset, something that had been taking place since the world began.

He studied her, fascinated despite his silent resolve not to be. Her features were lightly kissed by the rays that reached out long, spidery fingers one final time before the sun finally sank from view—only to begin the process all over again tomorrow night.

"Magnificent," he murmured in agreement. But he wasn't looking at the sunset.

The tone of Dan's voice slipped into her consciousness, drawing Tina's attention away from the sight she wanted him to appreciate.

Turning her eyes to his, Tina found that her breath instantly caught in her throat. The flippant remark that was all set to come out faded away, forgotten, evaporating without a trace.

When had the interior of the car gotten so small, so confining? So tight? They'd shared it on the way to Pine Ridge and now back and it hadn't seemed confining—until just this moment.

In contrast to the actual temperature, which was going down with the sun, after all this *was* the desert, the inside of the car grew quite warm.

When he leaned in closer, his fingertips skimming the outline of her cheek and then her chin, Tina was fairly certain that time stood still. At the very least, the earth had stopped spinning. Now it was her head that had taken on that task. All but spinning out of control.

All Tina could think of was touching her mouth to his.

Complications, her mind screamed in forewarning. If she let this happen, there would be tons and tons of complications.

Complications she should avoid, given that she would be interacting with the man on a daily basis and the town needed him. If things went sour, then he might leave and she would be responsible for that.

But right at this moment, she wanted nothing more than to have him kiss her. *Nothing.* Not life, not food, not a queen's ransom in jewels scattered at her feet, which related to a particularly dear dream she'd held on to as a child.

She wanted this man to kiss her.

Now.

Before she took matters into her own hands—literally—and kissed him.

Her heart hammered in anticipation.

It had been a long time since she'd sampled that kind of tenderness, a simple kiss between a man and a woman, and she ached for it the way a seedling ached to be bathed in the warmth of the sunlight.

He shouldn't be doing this, Dan upbraided himself. He was here to work, to attempt, in some small way, to take Warren's place, to do what Warren would have wanted to do. He was here because it was his fault that Warren wasn't.

He wasn't supposed to be giving in to urges and desires that had popped out of nowhere to plague him. Those kinds of reactions, of temptations, belonged to the man he'd been and perhaps, the man he would someday be again.

But he wasn't that man now.

Kissing her was asking for trouble. It was purely a selfish transgression, a breech of some unspoken covenant he'd made with Warren.

This was—

Absolutely unavoidable, a voice in his head whispered. If he was going to take another breath, it had to be one he'd draw in after he knew what her lips tasted like.

He *had* to find out.

Framing her face in his hands, holding it delicately and reverently, Dan leaned in and touched his lips softly to hers.

And immediately caused the earth to tilt ninety degrees off its axis, threatening by that very action to destroy the world as he now knew it. But it was worth it. Because he'd been right. Her lips *did* taste hopelessly sweet, like a treasured fruit, hidden in the recesses of the jungle.

Meaning to pull back, he wound up deepening the kiss, taking it from sweet and gentle to something more intense and filled with a passion the likes of which he couldn't remember ever encountering.

Whether that was a factor of the self-imposed celibacy he's been operating under or the woman he had allowed to slip in through the small crack in his world, he didn't know.

Dan needed to kiss her again to ascertain that.

So he did.

Chapter Eleven

An eternity later, Dan placed his hands on her shoulders and lightly, but firmly, pushed himself away.

With the contact severed between them, Tina took a deep, shaky breath, struggling to get herself, if not actually under control, at least to appear as if she was.

"Liked the sunset that much, did you?" she asked, doing her best to sound flippant and offhanded instead of a woman whose very foundation had suddenly and unexpectedly just been rocked.

"There was a sunset?" Dan deadpanned, maintaining such a straight face that at first she wasn't sure if he was being serious or not. And then the corners of his mouth softened just a little, taking on the semblance of a smile. He cleared his throat. "It's getting late. We'd better be getting back before someone sends out a search party for us."

That would be Miss Joan, Tina thought, since she'd made arrangements with the woman to pick up her son and bring him home. The woman wasn't an alarmist, but she did tend to worry unless informed about changes ahead of time.

Pressing her lips together, Tina nodded. Though she wouldn't say so out loud, she was grateful that Dan hadn't pushed what was clearly his advantage. For just a moment, she'd been on the brink of losing control, of being that girl who'd already wantonly given in to the sudden rush of heat mingled with desire in her veins.

She would have sworn that she'd come a long way from that girl she'd been, the one who'd so effortlessly succumbed to physical needs. The last time she'd done that, Bobby had been born nine months later. But since the accident and Don's death, she'd done a great deal of growing up. And withdrawing from that front.

Or so she'd thought.

Maybe not, she silently allowed, glancing at Dan's profile as he started up the car again to take them the rest of the way home.

Tina folded her hands in her lap and looked out the windshield, forcing her mind to go blank so she wouldn't be tempted to dwell on anything.

Easier said than done.

A week went by and neither one of them spoke about what had happened on the drive back from Pine Ridge. Not a single word. No reference whatsoever.

It became the elephant in the living room, forever in the way, reminding each of them of the one unguarded moment they'd shared.

For Tina it stirred up reams of questions. Had it been just a matter of going with the moment for Dan, or had he felt the same overwhelming pull? And if so, what was she supposed to do about it? Ignore it and stay safe? Explore it and risk everything?

What did it all mean?

Though she refrained from bringing the subject up and was grateful that he didn't, either, she knew damn well that she wasn't going to have a moment's peace until it was resolved. One way or another.

And then what? the little voice in her head demanded. *You sleep with him? We all know how that went for you the last time.*

It wasn't as if her track record or taste in men was above reproach—or even passingly decent. But all that was in the past and from everything she'd witnessed so far, Dan seemed to be a decent person. After all, he was out here, seemingly uninterested in making money from his patients. She'd been the one to charge his patients that first day, not Dan. He'd been seeing Forever's residents without making a single reference to the fact that he expected any form of payment from them.

Who does that but a saint?

At the very least, that was the height of selflessness. Something Don had never been, she thought ruefully. Not even on his best day.

There was no comparison between the two men. Don had been a user almost right from the start. Dan was here just to help because the people in Forever needed it.

A whole week had gone by. Seven long days in which he was achingly aware of the woman who sat out front, organizing his professional life. Booking his appointments, making certain that the flow of patients in and out of the medical clinic did not get out of hand.

He'd started something in that car on the way back from Pine Ridge. For both of them, Dan suspected. He hadn't meant to complicate their relationship, but he couldn't stop thinking about what had happened. While it didn't interfere with his being a doctor, it did interfere with his being a man. He had to stop examining this from every conceivable angle and just get on with life.

Forcing himself to come out of his haze, he glanced at his watch. It was past five. It occurred to him that Tina hadn't stuck her head in since the last patient had walked out of the office.

Was he finally done for the day?

If he was, maybe he and Tina could grab a bite of dinner together and then he'd ask her to go stargazing with him. After all, she'd been the one to bring it up in the first place. Alone with just the stars might be a good time to talk. Clear the air or some such trite saying, he mused.

Getting up from his desk, Dan walked out of his office. He was about to ask Tina if anyone else was left for him to see when the front door flew open, banging unceremoniously against the opposite wall.

On her feet, Tina froze the moment she saw who it was.

Rick.

Rick didn't even see her. His attention was focused on the only person he felt could help him. "Doc, I need you," he cried. "It's Olivia. I think the baby's coming. Now," he emphasized, trying to bank down the mounting fear in his voice.

Olivia was a couple of weeks shy of her due date, Tina

thought, but that could easily mean nothing. Then again, she knew it wasn't exactly unheard of to experience false labor pains. In either case, having a doctor around was not the worst idea.

"I'll just get my bag," Dan told the sheriff.

Ducking back into his office again, Dan hurried to retrieve the classic black bag that his uncle had given him when he'd graduated from medical school. Warren had received an identical one on his graduation.

When Dan returned to the reception area, there was no one there. Both Tina and the sheriff were outside, on either side of the woman in the service Jeep.

Tina opened the rear door closest to her. Peering in, she took Olivia's hand. In this one isolated instance, she was the one with experience and Olivia was the fearful novice.

It felt strange, she had to admit, albeit silently, to be on this side of the equation. Olivia had always been the one who was the rock, the steadfast person, the one *she* turned to if something was wrong, confident that Olivia could make it right.

"Hi, Livy," she said softly. "It'll be over with soon, I promise."

Olivia made no response. In the throes of a contraction, she wouldn't have been able to answer any sort of question. Despite the chill in the air, perspiration pasted her blond hair to her forehead.

"She wanted me to drive her to the hospital in Pine Ridge," Rick told both his sister-in-law and the approaching doctor, "but she looked like she was in too much pain to put up with the trip."

Dan drew in a long breath as discreetly as he could, then slipped into the car. The last time he'd been in the same room with a pregnant woman, she'd been a friend's wife and nowhere near ready to deliver. He didn't have much experience with delivering a child into the world. Without much experience to fall back on, he faced trial by fire. Unless Rick was exaggerating. Mentally, Dan crossed his fingers as he took Olivia's damp hand in his.

"So Rick tells me that you think you're about to have the baby."

Biting down on her lower lip, Olivia didn't trust herself to say a word. Instead, she nodded vigorously, her head bobbing up and down. Her hair remained almost immovable, pasted not just to her forehead but her cheeks, as sweat poured out each time a contraction seized her. Which was far too often now. There was no longer any time to rest, to regroup between assaults.

"How far apart are the contractions?" Dan asked, looking to Rick for an answer.

But it was Olivia who spoke. "Sixty," she squeezed out through lips that hardly moved.

"Every sixty minutes?" Dan repeated. Now that was more like it. The emergency scaled back. "Then we have enough time to get you to the hospital—"

Grabbing his hand back, Olivia held on for dear life, channeling the contraction from herself to Dan via her viselike grip.

"No," she cried desperately, struggling mightily to carry on the semblance of a coherent conversation when everything inside of her was being ripped to shreds. "Sixty *seconds*."

Dan reconnoitered. "Okay, we *don't* have time to get to the hospital." Managing to reclaim his thoroughly crushed hand, Dan backed out of the rear seat and turned toward Rick.

"I'm at least going to need to get her into the clinic," he told Olivia's husband.

Nodding, Rick coaxed his wife to the edge of the seat and then scooped her up. "You're a little heavier than I remember," he teased, trying to lighten the moment.

"I'm…hoping…to drop…twenty-five…pounds… soon," she answered, trying very hard to elude the next sharp, hard salvo of pain.

Dan hovered about his patient, prepared to make a grab for her. He was afraid that any second she might lapse into a contraction, stiffening enough to run the risk of having her husband drop her.

Tina led the way back into the building. She threw open one door after another until they were in the first exam room.

As gently as he could, Rick placed Olivia down on the examining table the way the doctor indicated.

After dropping his medicine bag on the first available empty surface, Dan quickly washed his hands and turned his attention back to his patient. One look at her expression told him that she hadn't exaggerated about the amount of time between contractions. If anything, she'd overestimated it. It seemed to him there were less than forty-five seconds between them now.

"This'll be over with very soon," Dan promised

her, offering the woman as much encouragement as he could.

"Not…soon…enough!" Olivia attempted to smile but what came through looked more like a grimace than a smile.

"Tina, get me a—"

Dan abruptly stopped. Anticipating his next move, Tina was way ahead of him.

Tina had already retrieved a sheet to drape over Olivia's soon-to-be exposed section for the purposes of modesty, even though when it came down to the wire, modesty was the first thing to go. Getting help and finally giving birth were far more important.

Spreading the sheet out over Olivia's lower half, she quickly got Olivia ready, taking off her sister's shoes, her maternity slacks and her underwear. Finished, she backed away, allowing Dan to step in so that he could make the proper assessment.

When he did, his face paled slightly.

"What's the matter?" Rick demanded.

"The baby's breech," Dan said.

"What does that mean?" Rick demanded.

"It means that the baby can't come out the way it is," Dan answered. "We're going to have to get her to the hos—" His words were lost as Olivia screamed.

Dan closed his eyes, centering himself. There was still a small chance she could have the child naturally. He looked at Olivia, his eyes on hers. "I'm going to have to try to turn the baby," he told her.

"You can do that?" Tina asked.

He didn't know. Saying so out loud would only cause

Olivia and her husband to panic, so he didn't answer. Instead, he warned Olivia, "This is going to hurt."

"Like...it...doesn't...now?" she questioned breathlessly.

"Sorry," was all he could say. "Hold her," he instructed Rick. When Rick closed his arms around his wife, Dan got started and thanked his lucky stars for having some training.

Praying, he took a firm hold of the infant's form and then, with great effort, slowly turned it just enough for the baby to emerge from the birth canal.

"Stay with me, Olivia, stay with me," Dan ordered, seeing that the woman was close to passing out. "We're almost— There!" he announced. It was done. Letting out a huge, shaky breath, he offered Rick a smattering of a smile. "Worst is over."

"Obviously, you've never given birth," Tina said under her breath.

But before Dan could say anything to her, the baby began its final descent.

Almost as exhausted as his patient, Dan murmured reassuring words to the woman. "Push when I tell you," he instructed. "All right, *push!*"

Mentally, he took it to the count of ten, then told her to stop. Panting, she slumped against Rick who still held her.

Wanting to distract her from what he could see was another contraction approaching, Dan asked, "Do you know what you're having?"

"An...elephant," Olivia expelled the words between clenched teeth. "A...great...big...fat...elephant!"

"Girl elephant or boy elephant?" Dan asked.

"We wanted to be surprised," Rick answered for Olivia. He was almost as breathless as she was, going through the ordeal vicariously. It was obvious by his expression that he felt every single pain along with his wife. "What can I do, Doc?"

"Just keep on supporting her shoulders like that when she pushes," Dan encouraged. The last word was no sooner out of his mouth when he saw Olivia beginning to bear down. "Not yet, not yet," Dan said quickly. "I want you to do it on my count. Nice, short, panting breaths, Olivia," he coaxed gently. "Just remember, you can't pant and push at the same time. It's a physical impossibility."

Again, he was grateful for his education, which had prepared him for just such an emergency. Olivia wasn't the only one he was trying to reassure. Silently, he was doing the same with himself.

At that moment, as the focus was on Olivia and the child who was fighting so hard to enter the world, music began to fill the air. Specifically, a song that had been climbing up the charts around this time a year ago.

Hearing it, it still took Tina a moment to make the connection. That was *her* cell phone that was ringing. Pulling the device out of her pocket, she snapped open the clam shell and put it to her ear, impatience streaming through her.

"Hello?" she snapped.

"Is everything all right over there?" It was Miss Joan and she sounded more than a little concerned. "Lupe said she saw the sheriff streaking by on his way to the clinic. She thought someone was in the backseat. Is it Olivia?"

Nothing ever got by that woman, Tina thought. As it was, she was glad Miss Joan called. She needed the woman to watch her son for a while longer. "Yes. She's having the baby right now. Could you—"

Tina didn't get a chance to finish.

"Don't give it another thought. Bobby and I will be playing games until his mama comes home. But if you don't get back in time for his bedtime, I'll tuck him in," Miss Joan assured her. "You just go help that sister of yours. She needs you. The first time's always the scariest for a woman."

She made it sound as if she knew firsthand, Tina thought. She wondered if Miss Joan *did* have any children of her own stashed away. But she would ask her at another time. Olivia needed her now, if only to be there and show her support. Tina fervently wished she could do more, but everything that could be done was up to the doctor.

"Thanks," she murmured to the woman on the other end of the line. Knowing that Bobby was being taken care of allowed her to focus her attention exclusively on her sister.

The thought that she was lucky to live in a place like this flashed through her mind once again.

Terminating the call, she slipped the phone back into her pocket.

Guttural sounds escaped through lips that appeared to be pressed together as Olivia, once more urged by Dan to push, bore down and pushed for all she was worth.

Pushed and had nothing to show for her efforts except a clear-down-to-the-bone exhaustion.

Exhaling, struggling desperately to suck in enough air to sustain herself and keep from passing out, Olivia once again fell back against Rick's strong hands. At this point, she was almost boneless in her exhaustion.

"It's never coming out," Olivia cried almost despondently.

Concern was etched into Rick's face as he looked at Dan. It was apparent that this was an Olivia he was unfamiliar with. Olivia Blayne Santiago was nothing if not feisty and a born fighter. Definitely *not* someone who gave in to despair.

"Should she be getting a C-section?" Rick asked.

Dan shook his head. He knew how much Olivia wanted to give birth naturally so he wasn't about to go that route unless he absolutely had to—for her sake, not his own.

"We're getting ahead of ourselves," Dan counseled. "The baby's in a very good position now. It's almost here." His eyes once again met Olivia's. "You can do this," he told her. "Just a little longer. Hang on just a little longer. It's only going to be a few more—"

He didn't get a chance to finish his sentence. Olivia was arching again, her back forming one half of a parenthesis as she writhed in pain.

"Push, Olivia, push," he ordered.

To his surprise, she didn't. "I can't," she cried, exhausted.

Rick took over. Still behind her, his hands against her back, propping her up, Rick leaned forward, his lips against her ear. "C'mon, baby, push. You can do it. I know you can," he coached urgently. "Now push!"

"If I can do it, you can," Tina told her, joining in. "You were always the one who could do anything she set her mind to, remember?" She saw Olivia's eyes shift toward her. "Let's get this over with so that Bobby can have someone to play with closer to his own age than Miss Joan."

She succeeded in making Olivia laugh—and it mysteriously seemed to give her a second wind.

The next moment, riding the cusp of a contraction, Olivia bore down again and pushed. Pushed until there wasn't an ounce of strength left within her.

But there was no need for any more strength. With a lusty squall, Olivia and Rick's baby exploded into the world.

"What…is…it?" Olivia asked in a drained whisper, unable to even lift her head to see the baby that Tina had taken into her arms.

"The most beautiful baby girl the world has ever seen," Tina declared, her eyes shimmering with unshed tears and love.

"She looks just like her mother," Rick murmured to his wife, choking up as he bent over to kiss Olivia's damp forehead. "You did good, baby."

"Congratulations, Olivia. You have a healthy baby girl," Dan told his patient.

Moving his stool back, he rose. Only then did he realize that his knees felt just the slightest bit weak and fluid.

Stripping off the rubber gloves, he tossed them into

the wastebasket as he silently congratulated himself. He had just had his first successful solo delivery.

More and more, he began to understand why Warren had chosen this route. Not just to work with those whose access to medical services was limited, but to experience that indescribable high that came from being in the trenches, from seeing firsthand what being there, offering help and hope, meant.

He'd never felt quite so alive before—

Except perhaps, he silently amended, glancing over toward the trio, when he'd kissed Tina.

Chapter Twelve

Two minutes ago, Rick had been beyond elation. So in love with his brand-new, only minutes-old baby girl there was no way to properly measure it. No way to properly measure how much he was in love with his wife all over again, either.

And then the doctor had said that Olivia and the baby should go to the hospital at Pine Ridge in the morning and suddenly, everything felt as if it was crashing down around him.

Rick's face was a mask of concern as he forced the words out, his voice hardly above a hoarse whisper. "Is there something wrong?" Fear ate away at his gut as he waited for the doctor to answer.

Dan was quick to reassure him. "No, there's nothing wrong, but—"

Rick frowned. "Then why do you want Olivia and the baby to go to the hospital?" he asked.

The answer was simple. Because the hospital had equipment that Dan didn't. Because there were standard tests to perform that he couldn't. "To make sure that everything is as good as I think it is." Trying to look as positive as he could, Dan placed a comforting hand on the sheriff's shoulder. "Think of it as a standard checkup." He smiled at Rick. "Your wife is healthy, your daughter's healthy, I just want to make sure I didn't overlook anything."

"Don't give the doc grief, Sheriff. He's just got everyone's best interests at heart. Better to be safe than sorry, right, Doc?"

All three occupants in the exam room turned toward the sound of the low, dark bourbon voice. Miss Joan walked in, taking command of the room by her sheer presence.

Deep hazel eyes immediately focused on Forever's newest resident. Miss Joan's face softened and transformed into a wreath of smiles as she came forward.

"Oh, now, you two have *got* to get started on another one as soon as Olivia's a little stronger." Her approving glance swept over both parents. "You do absolutely beautiful work."

Having folded a sheet several times over, Tina had wrapped her new niece in it and was still holding her, remembering what it felt like holding Bobby when he had been only minutes old.

Miss Joan stopped beside her. "Let me hold her for a second," the woman urged. Very carefully, Tina transferred her precious bundle into Miss Joan's arms. The latter beamed and sighed as she gazed down at the infant. "You forget how little they are when they start out," Miss Joan murmured. Looking up at Olivia, she asked, "Got a name for her?"

Exhausted but radiant, Olivia shook her head. "Not

yet," she confessed. "I want to see what her personality's like before we give her a name."

"Sounds like a good idea to me," Miss Joan agreed, unable to tear her eyes away from the baby in her arms. Very gently, she began to sway. After a moment, the baby's huge blue eyes began to drift shut.

Though Rick's fears had begun to settle somewhat, he still appeared concerned. "You're absolutely sure there's nothing wrong?" he asked Dan.

One of the lessons that had been passed on to the physicians in his graduating class was not to guarantee anything. They were doctors, not gods and for the most part, he'd believed that. But he could see that, although Rick hadn't put it into so many words, he needed peace of mind after having gone through this emotion-draining experience with his wife.

And, Dan reasoned, most likely there *was* nothing wrong with either mother or infant. So he broke a cardinal rule. He gave Rick the guarantee the man was looking for.

"I'm sure. But I'd be behaving recklessly if I didn't tell you to take them in to be double-checked at the hospital. Nothing wrong with getting a clean bill of health from two sources," Dan told him. "But for now, I'd say you both need to get some rest—if your new daughter will let you," he added with a smile, lightly running the back of his hand along the infant's cheek. The baby stirred, but went on sleeping.

"I'd say you all do," Miss Joan told not only Olivia and Rick, but Tina and Dan, as well. But the bulk of her attention was on the newly minted family. "Which is why I'm going home with you," she told Rick. "I'll take care of the little princess for you tonight and you two can both get some sleep." Now her gaze took them both in. "And that's not up for debate."

Olivia and Rick exchanged glances and then Rick nodded and answered, "Sounds good to us."

Tina realized that she was both exhausted and wound up all at the same time. There was no other explanation why this question hadn't struck her the second she saw Miss Joan come in.

"Where's Bobby?" Tina asked.

Unfazed, Miss Joan said, "I took him back to Lupe when I realized what was going on and that Olivia and Rick here might need help." She gave Tina an encouraging smile. "Don't worry, Baby Girl, your son's in his glory, being looked after by half a dozen girls."

Ordinarily, Miss Joan's part-time waitress looked after Bobby on the days she didn't work at the diner. Lupe's younger sisters were all in school during the day. But not at this time at night. That assured Tina there would be no lack of eyes on the little boy.

"I figured you might want to get a little rest yourself tonight," Miss Joan suggested. It was no secret that the woman had a way of anticipating needs, of being more sharply intuitive than she appeared to be at first glance. "Consider it my gift to you." Still holding the baby and loving every moment of it, she turned toward Dan. "Is the new mama strong enough to be moved?" she asked.

Olivia appeared exhausted, but there was no reason to believe she couldn't sit in the car and be driven home. "I don't see why not—as long as she doesn't have to walk home."

As if in response, Rick scooped his wife into his arms and picked her up. "She doesn't have to walk at all. I'll take it from here."

Secure in his arms, Olivia sighed as she leaned her head against her husband's chest. Miss Joan, carrying the baby, followed closely behind the pair. He had noticed before she came in that the woman had removed the boxed infant seat from the trunk and set it up in Rick's car.

Dan brought up the rear for form's sake and to field any last-minute questions from either of the new baby's parents.

It wasn't until he saw Rick deposit his wife into the backseat and then round the hood to get into the driver's side while Miss Joan took the seat beside Olivia, securing the infant in the car seat, that he realized that someone was missing.

Tina.

Nevertheless, he remained where he was, waiting until Rick started the car and then pulled away. The moment the vehicle had put some token distance between them, Dan turned around and went back into the clinic.

It seemed almost eerily still compared to all the commotion that had taken place just a little while ago. Had Tina ducked out when he wasn't looking?

The reception area was empty. He made his way into the exam room where he'd welcomed Forever's newest citizen. That was where he found Tina. Olivia's sister was busy, putting things away and cleaning up.

She was running on charged energy, he thought. When had she gotten her second wind? And how could he get some?

"You don't have to do that," he told her, nodding at the sheets she'd stripped off the examination table.

"It's not going to straighten itself out," she told him matter-of-factly. Turning her attention to the pile of hand towels that had been discarded on the floor, she found her wrists being suddenly caught in midtask.

Stilling her hands with his own, Dan advised, "At least wait until morning. I think you did enough for one night."

"I didn't do anything," she protested. "If anyone did anything, it was Olivia. And you, of course," she added quickly, not wanting him to be insulted. "You were very good with her." And she was really grateful for that. "She was trying not to show it, but I know Olivia was afraid." Just as she had been when faced with giving birth. "You made it easy for her. Thank you," she added after a beat.

Dan shrugged off the compliment. "I was just there to catch the baby."

She fixed him with a look. There was modest and then there was just *too* modest. "You're forgetting that you were the one who turned the baby," she reminded him. Heaven only knows what condition Olivia would have been in if he hadn't been there.

Pausing, Dan debated whether or not to say more. But the situation had turned out well, so he saw no harm in making the admission now. "That was my first delivery."

Tina was aware of that. She assumed he was referring to his first delivery in Forever. But the look on Dan's face made her uncertain enough to ask. "You mean here, in Forever, right?"

"No, I mean at all," he told her. "I've never delivered a baby before by myself though I've assisted."

"I thought that doctors were supposed to know everything." She smiled coyly.

"Somehow, I didn't get enough experience in that area." He shrugged. But inside, he was still riding a high crest. "I didn't think it really made all that much of a difference, since I was set to become a radiologist."

"Well, after watching you in action just now, I would have to say that would have been a complete waste of some pretty impressive talent." Her eyes shone as she told him, "You looked like a natural."

While her words were flattering, he considered the source. "Thanks. But I suspect your range of experience with doctors isn't exactly all encompassing and knowledgeable."

That was true, Tina silently conceded, but that still didn't change things. "You don't have to take a bite out of every apple to know a good one when you taste it."

The moment the words were out of her mouth, Tina looked as bemused as he did. Maybe more.

"That's a pretty folksy adage," he observed.

"I know," she admitted. She shook her head. "I have no idea where that came from. I guess that means I'm finally turning 'native,'" she speculated. The thought made her smile rather than cringe with self-critical dismay, the way she knew it might have at the mere suggestion less than a year ago.

Nodding toward the rear of the clinic, she made a suggestion. "Why don't you go upstairs, Dan? I'll just stay here a little longer, finish what I'm doing." He was making no effort to go so she added, "Don't worry, I'll lock up for you when I leave."

She was surprised when Dan asked, "Do you have to leave?"

The question seemed so innocent, but it suddenly accelerated her heartbeat. Tina wasn't completely clear why. In the blink of an eye, she could almost *feel* her blood rushing through her veins, bathing her in a warmth that was all enveloping.

He meant nothing by that, Tina silently insisted, trying her best to cap the intense excitement building within her. It was just a throwaway line, nothing more. No reason to think he meant anything by it.

Still, she heard herself answering in a gentle, low voice, "No, I don't."

"Good, because I could use the company right about now." The incredible sense of satisfaction at being part of the birthing process still wove through him. He was much too keyed up to sleep.

At this point, nerves whirled through her and her fingertips had gone moist while her throat had turned drier than sand.

Taking a breath, telling herself to get a grip, she asked him, "Want to go stargazing? It's a good night for it."

The sky looked as if a celestial being had upended

an entire sackful of stars, scattering them through the heavens.

Dan didn't want to be outside with her. Outside there was always a chance of prying eyes watching them and right now, he wanted her all to himself. He wanted to be with her without having to wonder if their every move, their every word, would be scrutinized by someone from Forever.

"Maybe later," he replied. Taking Tina's hand in his own, creating a bond that felt almost surreally intimate, given that they stood in the middle of a room that had seen so much activity only moments before, Dan had a counterproposal for her. "You said something about going upstairs."

Yes, she had. But she'd meant for him to go up alone while she remained here, getting everything squared away for tomorrow. She'd intended for him to get some rest. If they both went upstairs, neither one of them would get any rest. Not for a very long time.

The thought made her smile.

"Yes I did," she answered quietly, waiting for him to make the next move.

His hand still linked with hers, Dan drew her over toward the rear of the clinic, where the stairs that led to the upper floor were located.

There was no hesitation on her part.

And with each step she took, her heartbeat accelerated a little more until, at the top of the landing, it did a drum solo.

He wanted to kiss her.

Had to kiss her.

Without taking another step toward his bedroom, Dan turned to face her again. His long, skillful fingers slipped into her hair, framing her face.

Bending his head ever so slightly, he kissed her. First softly, then with more and more feeling and intensity.

Just like the first time.

Tina could feel herself losing ground. The floor beneath her melted away, leaving her suspended in a nebulous place with no boundaries. A place from where, any second now, she would begin free-falling.

Her arms entwined around his neck, Tina leaned her soft, yearning body into his. The hard contact registered instantly and heightened her excitement tenfold, increasing the heat that soared through her. She stopped thinking. Desire took the helm, making gratification, and the man who could give it to her, her ultimate goal.

Her heart almost hurt, it raced so hard. She would have been seriously worried about the organ cracking a rib and breaking through her chest—if she could have linked her thoughts into a coherent whole. But there were no coherent thoughts, only fragments swirling around her brain.

Everything centered around Dan and only Dan. At this moment, the man was the beginning and the end and the middle. Of everything.

There was nothing else nor did she need there to be. Only him.

She lost herself in his kiss.

Tina became vaguely aware of moving again. Of being linked to Dan, with a desire roaring through her veins that she'd never experienced before.

Was it because she'd been deprived of any sort of male-female contact for the past ten months? Having made love before, was the absence enough to overwhelm her like this, to make her jump at the first man who tried to seduce her?

Somehow, she didn't think so.

These urges, these needs, hadn't hammered through her before. At least, not with this intensity. Not until his mouth had made her silent promises, pressed hotly against hers. The very taste of his lips made her drunk with pleasure.

Another new terrain crossed.

The last time he'd been with a woman was the afternoon before the car accident that had claimed Warren. Technically speaking, that wasn't really enough time to create this kind of a hunger within him.

Though he'd been far from a hermit after his very first venture into lovemaking, he'd never been the type of man who lived and breathed sex, who began to suffer from acute cravings after a certain number of days had gone by. None of his relationships lasted any real length of time, but they were still satisfying on more than just a single level.

Yet he'd never actually done this before. Never felt this level of involvement before. His body literally *ached* as he tried to get his fill of her. Every kiss just led to the next, each intimate pass of his hands along her body begged for another. For more.

An urgency slammed through him, starving for what his body instinctively knew waited for him down the line. All the while, he could feel the passion within him increasing. Growing at a prodigious rate.

Even so, he didn't want to take things for granted. Worse, he didn't want to overwhelm her, impose his will on her because right at this moment, he felt as if he'd combust if he couldn't have her.

But he wasn't about to take his fill, to satisfy himself at her expense.

Drawing his head back, Dan was vaguely surprised to see that they were no longer still in the hall, that they had somehow made their way to his bedroom.

And that he had her more than partially disrobed. When had that happened?

Moreover, he'd shed his shirt somewhere—or had she done that for him? And his jeans were probably lying in the same place that his shirt was.

It was then that he realized her cool, tapering fingers that played along his skin were causing an almost impossible wave of heat to sizzle along the length of his body.

"You're sure?" he asked, his voice hardly more than a low rumble.

He felt her smile before he saw it.

"This is a hell of a time to stop to fill in a questionnaire," she whispered, her voice achingly raspy.

"I want you to be sure."

There was something in the way he said it, a warning note in his voice, that for one moment, almost chilled her. What was he trying to say? Did he want to put her on notice—that no matter what happened, it was just for tonight?

She already understood that. Had not just made her peace with it but told herself she preferred it that way. If this was just an interlude, a fleeting aberration with no demands or expectations on either side, there would be no future breakup in the offing.

And no pain.

"This is just for tonight," she whispered, her lips brushing against his as she made the pronouncement. "Not forever."

If he wanted to say anything more, make any further disclaimer or ask her to sign an oath in blood, it never transpired. Because she shed the last of her clothing and pressed her near perfect, nude body against his. And instantly took him prisoner.

He went not only willingly but eagerly.

The next moment, any passion that was still bridled broke free.

A frenzy overtook them both, swallowing them up and leaving no trace. The caresses became more urgent, the kisses more powerful.

He made love to every inch of her, claiming each and every part and making it his.

At least for now.

The momentum built until she didn't think she could hold out much longer. And then, suddenly, he was there, fitting his hips against hers, becoming one with her. Moving in a rhythm that was almost faster than a heartbeat.

Tina clung to him, echoing his movements until the final, all encompassing moment when the blinding eclipse swallowed them whole, separating them from the rest of the world.

Chapter Thirteen

The descent back to earth, to reality, was slow, languid. Like a leaf floating on a gentle, summer breeze, making the journey from the top of an uppermost branch down to the soft, welcoming ground below.

Dan expected the exhilarating euphoria to fade and then disappear. The way it always had before.

Except this time, it wasn't disappearing or even fading.

This was something new. Something different. As he turned his body toward the woman lying beside him, he realized that this had a tenderness he'd never felt before. At this moment, trying to come to grips with what was happening, what *had* happened, he felt both ten feet tall and bulletproof as well as vulnerable as hell.

Maybe he was having some sort of a delayed emotional crisis or breakdown because of Warren's death. But the fact of the matter was it didn't feel like a breakdown. It felt…amazingly good.

He found himself wanting her again.

No. No, no, no, no, no, Tina silently and firmly admonished herself. She couldn't *let* herself feel this way, couldn't think of this as anything but a passing interlude. A wonderful, heart-racing, teeth-jarring interlude, but an interlude nonetheless.

Just because the man deserved an A plus-plus in love-making didn't change that. She couldn't allow herself to get involved with a technique. That was only just a part of him. The package was always the whole man and she already knew how very bad her taste in men was.

Hadn't she learned by now that she had a habit of letting her guard down with the wrong kind of man and then, before she knew it, she was practically an emotional prisoner? The last one had almost killed her. Wasn't that enough to teach her a lesson?

The last one had given her Bobby, a little voice whispered. Bobby, the brightest spot in her life.

But his conception had been an accident, she had to remember that. And, she reminded herself sternly, Don had been skilled at lovemaking, too. He'd known all the right moves, the right gestures.

But compared to Dan, Bobby's father had been an amateur, a hopeless, fumbling rookie.

That *still* changed nothing. She wouldn't let herself fall into that trap again, wasn't going to lead with her heart only to wind up taking it on the chin. Tonight had been very, very nice. Okay, *better* than nice. But that was the end of it. She just couldn't allow herself to get carried away, and as long as she remembered that, she would be safe.

Right?

Raising her eyes to his, she realized he was looking

at her. Almost scrutinizing her. What's more, he didn't seem pleased.

"You're frowning," she noted.

Was she that bad? Was he going over the other women he'd had to find her lacking? A man who looked like Dan had to have had a great many women. Tina braced herself for an explanation. And criticism.

"That's because I'm happy."

She blinked, confused. "You realize that doesn't make any sense, right? People don't frown when they're happy."

"They do when they shouldn't be."

"And you shouldn't be happy?" she asked, trying to understand.

"I shouldn't *be* at all," he told her in a sobering moment. Why did he get to be the one who was here tonight, enjoying this woman who, without trying, made his knees so weak? Why did he get to be the one to live and Warren the one to die?

In the face of his answer, and the incredibly sad look in his eyes, Tina forgot about her own insecurities, forgot that she was lying here beside him completely naked. In less than a moment, her attention—and concern— shifted to the man who had, quite literally, rocked her world. The man whose sadness now tore at her heart.

"You're going to have to explain that to me," she urged him.

With one hand tucked in beneath her, Dan rolled onto his back and looked up at the ceiling without saying a word.

The silence stretched out between them until Tina

was convinced that he had no intention of telling her what he'd meant. And then, just as she was about to try to coax an answer out of him, in a low, quiet voice that was carefully scrubbed of all telltale emotion, Dan began to talk.

"I should have been the one who died in that car accident, not Warren. He should be here now, in Forever, not me." If there was any justice, he should be lying in a grave, Dan added silently.

"Warren," Tina repeated, her mind scrambling to link things up. "That was your brother, right?"

He nodded. Then, as emotion began to fill his voice despite his efforts, he propped himself up on his elbow and looked at her. Looked at her face. Searching for understanding. Maybe even for a little absolution, he wasn't sure.

"Warren wasn't just my brother, he was my best friend."

His mouth curved slightly as he remembered bits and pieces of their lives together. They'd made the journey through medical school and residency together, Warren, the exceptionally smart one and he, the playboy. But they were a team. Always a team. And now, because of him, there was no team.

"We were as different as night and day, but we had each other's backs. At least, he always had mine." And he had let Warren down. If he'd been more in tune with Warren and stopped thinking only of himself, he would have let his brother stay in the apartment that night. And remain alive. "Warren didn't want to come out that night. He wanted to spend a quiet, final evening in the apartment, packing, getting ready. Talking. I convinced him—forced him really," he corrected ruefully, "to come out with me 'one last time.'"

His face paled and took on a haunted look as Dan relived the last few hours he'd had with Warren.

"God, if I'd only known how prophetic those words would be." A ragged breath escaped his lips. "We were in a taxi, going back to the apartment after a long night of celebrating, when a van came out of nowhere, ran the light and just plowed into the taxi. I got a bump on the head, the taxi driver was rushed to the hospital because he was critically injured and Warren, Warren got his wings." The smile twisted his lips, Tina noted, and it did not reach his eyes. "At least, that was what he'd always believed. That things don't just end here. That they continue someplace else."

She nodded, finding herself in agreement with a man she could never meet. "And you came here to take his place."

Dan laughed shortly. "No one could take Warren's place," he told her. And then he shrugged helplessly. "The best I can do is just try."

Compassion filled her. Tina placed a hand gently on his shoulder in mute comfort. "Don't be so hard on yourself," she said gently. "The people around here think the world of you and every one of them feels you've made a difference in their lives just by being here. A huge difference. Imagine, if you hadn't been here tonight, who knows what sort of complications Olivia might have had? We both know that contrary to popular opinion, giving birth is not like falling off a log. That baby might have died. You saved her," she insisted firmly. "Cut yourself a little slack," she urged. "You have every right to be happy, Dan."

As she spoke, she cupped his cheek with her hand, wishing she could erase the torment in his eyes. "Give yourself permission to be happy."

Stirred, mesmerized by the compassion he saw in her eyes, Dan took her hand and turned it over so that her palm faced him. He gently pressed a kiss to the soft flesh.

Arousing her.

Arousing himself.

He tried to tell himself that he was only having a purely physical reaction to her, nothing more. That it was just his sexual appetite that was stirring. If he was aware of anything more, he ignored it because he was afraid to make that admission, even to himself. Afraid of what it might mean and where it might lead him.

And despite what she maintained, Dan still felt that he had no right to be happy. Not when, in his own eyes, he was the one responsible for his brother's untimely death. But he was still grateful for the comfort that she offered. Grateful to be able to lose himself in her and receive solace, even for a moment.

Releasing her hand, he moved on to her throat, kissing the sensitive skin along the side. Creating havoc within himself. His heart lunged in his chest as he pulled Tina to him and began to make love to her all over again. As if it was the first time.

LIFE DIDN'T GET BACK to normal. Oh, the sun was still where it was supposed to be and so was the moon, but things were different now. *Felt* different now. After that first time, they each found excuses to face the end of the day in each other's arms, whether she was with him at the clinic or he with her in some out-of-the-way place they stole away together. Tina would call Miss Joan to explain that she had to work a little late, asking her to babysit Bobby a little longer for her.

She'd hear the woman laugh knowingly and agree. Telling Miss Joan that it really *was* work never carried any weight so she gave it up.

But even as they made the world stand still in each other's arms, Tina tried to resist what went on within her. Resist letting herself get carried away.

She *couldn't* allow herself to take Dan's words to heart, or make more of what had transpired between them. They'd merely had a completely exhilarating love-making experience.

But it was hard for her to stay grounded when some-how, he'd managed to tunnel his way into her heart. It hadn't been his lovemaking, magnificent though it was, that had gotten him trespasser rights to her heart. It was the pain she saw in his eyes. They had something in common. Because, in his own way, Tina felt that Dan was as wounded a soul as she was.

No matter what she told herself to the contrary, her resolve disintegrated the moment she was around him. And she was around him at least eight hours a day on a normal work basis—and that didn't take into account the time they spent together after hours. She found that her determination to keep both her feelings and Dan at arm's length was as firm as a stick of butter left out in ninety-degree heat. She melted every time.

She was her own worst enemy. Their nights of love-making were vividly stored in her memory banks, ready to pop up when she least expected them. They colored absolutely everything else in her life.

Stern lectures to the contrary, she'd never been happier. Every so often, she'd look up from what she was doing and catch Dan watching her. Just watching her. And smiling. Instantly, she'd feel warmth washing over her, laying siege to her.

In her heart, she knew that given her past, her relationship with Dan was doomed to fail. He seemed perfect, but there was no such thing. Eventually, the flaws would surface and one of them would be the fatal one. The beginning of the end.

She had to protect herself, protect her heart. She couldn't get so wound up around this man that she fell apart when the end came, as it inevitably would. She had Bobby to think of and he needed her.

But there was a huge difference between her plan and what she actually did. Determined not to lead with her heart, she was still doing it.

Don't panic, she counseled herself more than once. *Just for now, see where it goes. You can always bail out later.*

Right. As if it was that easy, Tina silently mocked herself.

For his part, Dan wrestled with his own conscience. He felt guilty for being happy. He felt equally guilty for leading Tina on. She wasn't the kind of girl to just have a fling. She was the permanent, nesting kind. And he wasn't going to stay.

He hadn't said as much, hadn't told anyone, not even Miss Joan, that his time in Forever was finite. That he was only here until another doctor could be found to take his place. Everyone in town thought he'd relocated here permanently and he hadn't set them straight. Hadn't told anyone that it was a lie.

Something else to feel guilty about, Dan thought with a heavy sigh, as he sat at his desk, staring down at his last patient's folder.

Rousing himself, he completed making notes in Annie Farmer's file. After closing the folder, he pushed it aside on his desk and rose from his chair. When he came out of his office, he saw that the doors of both examination rooms were open. Which meant that they were unoccupied.

Curious, Dan walked out into the reception area only to find it empty. Tina was at her desk, her fingers flying across the keyboard. Looking more compelling than anyone had a right to be.

He came up behind her and lightly placed his hands on the back of her chair. He caught just the slightest whiff of her perfume and felt his gut tightening in anticipation. How had this woman gotten to him so fast? This had never happened to him before and the timing couldn't have been worse.

"No patients?" he asked.

Tina automatically saved what she was typing as she turned her head to look at him. Her heart just had to stop leaping every time she saw him, or heard his voice. Or thought about him.

It was beginning to seem hopeless.

Finding her voice, she said, "I think you cured everyone. Looks like, barring someone bursting through the door—" the way her brother-in-law had three weeks ago "—we can go home early."

Dan glanced at his watch. It was a quarter to five. "Not exactly like getting half a day," he commented. "Want to grab some dinner?" he asked, trying his best to sound nonchalant.

What he really wanted to "grab" wasn't on any menu, but at least this way, he'd have her company and if they were in full view of everyone, he didn't have to worry about being tempted or experiencing a breakdown in his resolve. There would be too many witnesses around for him even to lightly brush his lips against hers.

Tina smiled and for the umpteenth time he was struck by how she seemed to light up the entire room every time her mouth curved.

"I'd like that," she told him. "I have to swing by the diner anyway. Lupe and the others are taking care of Bobby jointly today."

Olivia had been Bobby's main caretaker, sharing duties with the waitresses at the diner only when she was out on calls. But since her sister had had her own baby, Tina thought it only fair to leave her lively little firecracker with someone more up to being able to handle him right now. For the time being, Olivia had her hands full learning how to be a full-time mother—and the learning process could be overwhelming.

Familiar with the situation, Dan nodded. Yesterday he'd done something he would have never dreamed of doing. He paid an actual house call. He stopped by Olivia's house to do a routine check on her and the baby. While doing well, Tina's sister wasn't up to anything very strenuous yet. And as he'd observed, caring for Tina's son could, at times, be exceedingly strenuous. Just a little more than one, Bobby was very advanced for his age. Fueled by energy and curiosity, he got into literally everything.

"I've got an idea," he said. "Why don't you bring him here with you tomorrow?"

She looked at him, stunned. And then her smile grew even wider. Even more warming. "You wouldn't mind?" she asked.

Ordinarily, telling someone it was all right to bring their baby to the office wouldn't have even occurred to him. And, under those circumstances, if it had been suggested by someone else, he would have vetoed it. But this wasn't an upscale hospital in the middle of one of the most urban cities in the world. This was a small medical clinic in Forever. A diminutive, almost fairy tale-like town that was nothing if not laidback and relaxed.

As it was, every morning when he woke up and came downstairs to the clinic, part of him half expected the theme song from *The Andy Griffith Show* to begin playing the moment the first patient walked through the door. Having a little boy in the office getting into everything somehow seemed in keeping with the atmosphere.

"I wouldn't have suggested it if I minded," he told her. "Ready?"

Switching off her computer, Tina rose to her feet. Her eyes smiled at him. "Ready."

"WELL, LOOK WHO'S HERE," Miss Joan declared as Dan walked in with Tina. She turned around to look at the clock on the wall. "And early, too. Run out of sick people?" she asked with a throaty laugh.

"For now," Dan answered. He and Tina each took a seat at the counter. "Got any of that cherry pie left over from yesterday?"

"For you?" Reaching over, Miss Joan patted his hand. "Always. Saved you a piece," she said with a wink, then pretended to become stern. "But you're not getting it until you've had your dinner."

She was acting like a mother. It felt really odd, at this point in his life, after having done without one for so long. But he knew the woman meant well.

"Whatever you say, Miss Joan." He didn't bother looking at the menu propped up in front of him, tucked against the napkin dispenser and the salt and pepper shakers. It was easier to go straight to the source. "What looks good tonight?"

Miss Joan smiled wickedly. "She's sitting right next to you."

Could the woman be more obvious? Tina thought, struggling to keep a flush of color from creeping up her cheeks. "Miss Joan," she hissed, a warning look in her eyes.

The older woman merely shrugged, unfazed by the embarrassed reproach in Tina's voice. "Just stating the obvious, Baby Girl. He did ask," Miss Joan pointed out. "And I call 'em as I see 'em."

"How about the fried chicken?" Dan asked, wanting to spare Tina any more embarrassment. "Is that any good?"

Miss Joan squared her shoulders. "Doc, it's *always* good," she informed him. "Nobody ever came away from my diner complaining about the food." She tossed her head. Her red hair, weighed down with hair spray, remained perfectly stationary. "It's just a matter of degrees of good," she added.

"And where does the fried chicken come in on that chart?" Dan asked.

"Right at the top," Miss Joan said without hesitation. The recipe for the chicken was her own and she was quite proud of it.

"Okay, fried chicken it is," Dan said.

Tina slipped the menu back into its place. She'd taken it out of habit. It gave her something to do. "Make that two," Tina told the older woman.

"Love seeing young people agree," Miss Joan confided. Making the proper notation on her order pad, she tore off the sheet and placed it on the counter for the short order cook in the rear of the diner to pick up.

"I'm sorry about that," Tina murmured under her breath the moment the other woman had turned away. "I don't know what's gotten into her." She didn't bother to mention that the other evening, Miss Joan had extolled all of *his* virtues for a good half hour.

"Don't give it another thought. Some people feel they're born matchmakers." One of his friends' mothers when he was in medical school had felt she had the calling. She'd tried to match him up several times before she finally gave up. "Her choice could have been a lot worse," he added. "At least for me."

Tina felt his eyes slide along her body and found herself struggling not to blush again, even as her body hummed in anticipation of the night that lay ahead.

Chapter Fourteen

Tina was amazed how much her life had changed in a short space of time. From the middle of July to now, the end of September.

Ten weeks.

Dr. Dan Davenport had been part of her life and part of Forever for the past ten weeks. Not exactly a huge amount of time unless measured in seconds. But then, it felt as if he'd been part of her life forever.

It felt as if she'd suddenly come to life in that space of time, she reflected with a smile as she sat down at her desk and switched the computer on to start her work day. For the first time, she was really alive as a woman.

Oh, she'd be lying if she didn't admit that tiny smattering of fear still lingered within her. Having been with someone like Don made trusting another man not exactly the easiest thing to accomplish. Every now and then, that old fear would raise its head, whispering, *What if you're wrong? What if Dan isn't what he seems? What if he breaks your heart just like Don did? Can you stand it again?*

The answer was no, because this time, though she'd

tried very hard to stop it, her heart was invested all the way. She'd done a lot of thinking, a lot of weighing, before allowing herself to surrender her heart. This time, because of all the initial hesitation and soul-searching, Tina knew she loved that much harder. That much more completely.

This time, she'd committed to love as an adult, someone who'd been around a time or two. She wasn't that wide-eyed kid anymore, she was a woman, a mother, and that made all the difference in the world.

This commitment, she'd silently promised herself, was the one that would stick.

And, in that very same heart that had been so reluctant to open up, she *knew* that Dan felt the same way about her. Oh, he hadn't come out and *said* the words, but he'd come close. He'd told her that she made him happy and when he looked at her, she felt everything light up inside. You didn't feel like that, didn't have that kind of a connection, with someone who didn't *care* about you.

As for her, she'd come close to telling him she loved him several times in the past couple of weeks. As recently as last night, the words had hovered on her tongue. But she'd forced herself to hold them back. That was one area where she was old-fashioned. She wanted Dan to say "I love you" first. The last thing she wanted was for him to echo the words only because she'd said them to him. Or worse, not say anything at all.

All he had to do was to tell her he loved her and her own emotions would come pouring out.

For now, it was worth the wait. Blinding happiness

always was, she thought, thinking of her parents' marriage. Her parents had not only loved each other but had remained *in* love until the day they died. And she could see that Olivia and Rick loved each other a great deal. It was all there for the world to see, in the small, everyday details of living.

She wanted that and she knew now that it was out there for her.

Or rather, in here for her, she thought as she heard Dan coming down the back stairs. With no one else in the medical clinic to offer a distraction, she was able to make out the sound of Dan's shoes with their hard heels hitting the stairs and then the wooden floors as he approached the front of the clinic.

She smiled to herself. If the man was going to be a Texan and not a New Yorker, she would have to work on his Western makeover. First thing he needed was a pair of boots.

She tried to picture him in just that—and maybe a Stetson—and her smile widened considerably.

Dan paused to glance around as he came into the reception area from the rear.

"No patients yet?" he remarked, surprised and oddly pleased. It would be nice to take the day at a slower pace than he'd been doing.

"Haven't unlocked the front door yet," Tina pointed out, putting the first few files out on the side of her desk. "You still have fifteen minutes before your office hours start."

His hand on the back of her chair, he turned her around, bent his head down and brushed his lips against hers. His eyes were pure mischief as he regarded her closely.

"Fifteen minutes, huh? There's fresh paper covering the exam tables," he told her, an incredibly sexy, come-hither smile on his lips.

Tempted though she was, Tina knew that once she got started, everything else would be blocked out—and what if a patient came knocking on the door early? Then what?

So when he took her hand, she gently pulled it away while shaking her head. "Oh, no, I want much more than just fifteen minutes with you," she answered, a wicked grin taking the place of her innocent smile.

Dan laughed, amused. "Ah, the woman's getting greedy now, is she?"

"The 'woman' doesn't want to just settle for crumbs," she countered.

"Crumbs is it?" he echoed, giving her a longer, deeper kiss before backing away. "Did that feel like a crumb?" he challenged.

She struggled to catch her breath and then forced herself to gulp in air. "No," she managed to say with a tiny bit of dignity. "It didn't."

Satisfied, he backed away. She was, after all, right. Something told him that if he got started making love with her, he wasn't going to want to keep one eye on the clock—*or* stop that soon. "But your point is well-taken," he admitted. "Besides, it gives me something to look forward to at the end of the day."

She would have said, "Me, too," if she hadn't found herself suddenly wanting him with an urgency that all but took the rest of her breath away. Each time they made love, she just wanted Dan that much more.

Was that normal? she wondered, then decided she didn't care if it was or not. Feeling this was wonderful and that was all that counted to her.

About to ask him a question regarding his preference about billing statements, she stopped abruptly when someone began pounding on the front door.

Looking toward the urgent sound, Dan commented, "I thought you told me that I still had fifteen minutes before we opened."

"Fourteen now," Tina automatically corrected, walking to the door. "And you do."

Pushing the curtain away from the side window, she was about to tell whoever it was to calm down and wait. But the instant she saw the frantic face of Jacob Lyons, she flipped back the lock and opened the door. The retired ranch hand, who now made a living as the town's all around handyman, was not one to get alarmed easily and he clearly looked that way now.

"You gotta come, Doc," he declared without preamble. "I think he broke his leg or something."

Jake turned around and was about to lead the way back. Thinking fast, Dan caught hold of the wiry man's shoulders to keep him anchored in place.

"Hold it. *Who* broke his leg?"

Even as he asked, Dan had the uneasy feeling the cowboy could be talking about a horse. From what he'd heard, the man tended to be closer to horses than most of the people in Forever. The town vet, Mona, the sheriff's sister, was out of town for several days. But that didn't mean that he could jump in, despite the fact that some people around Forever thought that a doctor was a doctor and that a vet and a regular doctor could do the other's job in a pinch.

To his relief, Jake was talking about a person.

"Murphy. George," he clarified in case there was some doubt. "Nobody's heard from him in days so I went over. Had to almost break down the door—" He grew impatient to get going. "I can tell you all this on the way over," he urged.

There might be some reason for concern at that, Dan thought. George Murphy was getting on and he was not in prime condition. "Tina, get my bag, please," he requested, then added, "And hold down the fort until I get back."

Moving quickly, Tina was in and out of the medical clinic faster than anyone he'd ever seen. Had to be some kind of a record, he mused. Jake had barely gotten out three incoherent sentences in the time it had taken Tina to make the round-trip in and out of the clinic to get his bag.

He also noticed that she'd pulled the door firmly shut behind her.

"Nothing in the fort to hold down," she informed him. The patients, when they arrived, could just wait out here for the time being. "And if you think I'm not coming with you, you don't know me."

"But I'm willing to learn," he murmured to her. Opening the door of his sedan, he turned to look at the man beside him. He gestured for him to get into the back. "Okay, Jake, let's go see if we can find George."

At the time, it was said to humor the older man. But once they arrived before George Murphy's small, wood-framed two-story house and he opened the front door, Dan realized that finding his patient might actually not be the easiest of missions to accomplish.

"What *is* this?" Dan asked, stunned as he found himself looking at mounds of what appeared to him to be junk. Three and four and five feet high piles of things that were hard or completely impossible to identify, or utterly useless pieces of junk.

Miss Joan had told her all about George Murphy shortly after she and Olivia had returned to Forever. The man's house brought out the industrial cleaner in her.

"The accumulation of a lifetime," Tina told him. "Mr. Murphy's never been known to throw anything out, at least not willingly," she added.

"I make him throw things out every month," Jake announced proudly, wading into the virtual filth. "But somehow, he always seems to bring twice as much in." There was more than a note of frustration in his voice.

Dan nodded. "A hoarder."

Jake stopped, as if he couldn't believe what he'd just heard. "Did you just call him a whor—"

Dan quickly cut him off. "No, a hoarder," he enunciated carefully. "That's someone who keeps unnecessary, useless things no one else wants, saying that they might come in handy sometime."

The hoarding was done to unconsciously feed a deep psychological need to feel insolated and protected from the world, but Dan judged that might be more information than Jake needed to hear or absorb right now.

Jake nodded his head solemnly. "Yeah, that. A hoarder," he repeated. "That's George all right."

"It's a medical condition," Dan informed the former ranch hand. A condition he'd never encountered firsthand until just now, he thought. "It's a form of OCD—"

"Obsessive-compulsive disorder," Tina explained. She saw the stunned look on Dan's face. "I've been reading up on medical terms," she told him. She was doing it in an effort to be more of a help to him, more a part of his world. The pleased expression that came over his face told her that she was succeeding.

"Yeah, whatever you say," Jake mumbled dismissively. "But I heard him yell out in pain when I came looking for him this morning and opened the door."

"Why didn't you try to find him?" Tina asked.

"Couldn't. Didn't want to waste time, not with George screaming like he was being gutted, so I came to get the doc," Jake answered.

Cocking his head, Dan listened. And heard nothing. "I don't hear anything now," he said, turning toward Jake. "What makes you think he broke his leg?"

Jake looked at him as if he'd just asked a simpleton question. "'Cause he was yelling out, 'my leg, my leg, it's busted.'"

"That would definitely be a clue," Tina agreed, the corners of her mouth curving as she looked at Dan.

It would have been funny under other circumstances. But Murphy was no longer yelling. He might have passed out from the pain—or from blood loss, in which case the situation was critical. Dan looked around at the debris. He'd never encountered anything remotely like this. And it was damn near overwhelming.

"He could be anywhere."

"Murphy, can you hear me?" Jake shouted. When there was no answer, he raised his voice, cupping his hands around his mouth. "Murphy. George Murphy! Can you hear me?"

"He might have passed out from the pain," Tina suggested.

Dan looked at her and realized she was aware of the other alternative but hadn't said it to spare Murphy's friend. Dan started to say something, then stopped. He held his hand up to keep anyone from talking as he cocked his head to listen more closely.

He could have sworn he'd heard a faint cry. Another one followed on its heels, a little louder, a little more filled with pain.

"I hear it, too," Tina told him, answering the silent question in his eyes.

"I think it's coming from over there." Dan pointed to a particularly cluttered section.

Pushing through the mounds of rotting newspapers and discarded garbage like someone making his way through impeding everglade waters, Dan followed the sound of the man's cries. Jake and Tina were right behind him. Excited, Jake managed to circumvent Dan and the older man took the lead.

"Murphy, are you in there? It's me, Jake!" Jake called out.

Entering a room that appeared to have even more

piles of debris than the first, all kinds of boxes and papers, Dan saw a freestanding bookcase that was no longer standing. It was over on its side, as if unable to put up with its weight. However, it appeared to still be half-filled with books.

When they came closer, they saw that the bookcase was also pinning George Murphy's lower torso down beneath it.

"Dr. Livingston, I presume," Dan heard himself mumbling as he pushed closer to the man. He bent down to press his fingers to the man's neck to check for a pulse.

Murphy's eyes fluttered open.

"Hell, no, that's Murphy," Jake told the doctor. Squatting down beside his friend, Jake asked, "What the hell are you doing on the floor like that?"

"Wasn't my idea," the other man snapped, coming to fully. "Damn thing just decided to fall over."

"Might have something to do with it being perched on a mound of papers in the first place," Tina pointed out tactfully. Her words were ignored by the two older men as if she'd never spoken them.

"What time is it?" Murphy demanded.

"Almost nine o'clock," Tina replied, looking at her watch.

"Damn it, I've been here since last night." Murphy looked accusingly at his friend. "What took you so long?"

Jake didn't answer. Instead, while Dan and Tina worked together to raise the bookcase off his lower half, Jake angled his arms underneath Murphy's and managed to drag the man back enough to be free of the weight. Murphy yelled out in pain throughout the entire ordeal.

"You're going to raise the dead," Jake accused.

"As long as I ain't joining them." Murphy snapped. He bit his lower lip to keep from yelling out again.

A quick exam told Dan that Murphy had been right in his unprofessional assessment. The man's left leg was broken. At the very least, the man would need a cast. But first they needed to get him to the clinic—and out of here.

"I need to make a splint," he told Murphy.

"Do whatever you have to, just make it stop," Murphy groaned. He was sweating profusely at this point.

"Think you can find me two straight sticks and some tape or rope?" Dan asked Jake.

"Hell, give me enough time and I'd probably be able to find Dallas in here," Jake quipped, rising unsteadily to his feet. They were planted on an uneven mound of papers.

"Sticks and tape'll do," Dan said.

"Wiseass," Murphy grumbled, then looked almost sheepish as his eyes slid over toward Tina. "Sorry."

Tina waved the apology away. "You're not yourself right now, Mr. Murphy," she said, absolving him.

Within minutes, Jake came stumbling back with his find. He held out what appeared to be two yardsticks, the origin of which were anyone's guess. He also had a huge ball of twine. "This do?"

Dan took the items from him. "They'll do just fine,"

he assured Jake. "Tina, hold these in place for me just like this," he asked, buffering Murphy's leg.

Squatting beside Dan, a sense of pleased purpose wove through her as she did as he asked. This, she couldn't help thinking as she glanced at his profile while Dan worked, was the way things were supposed to be. Her whole life felt as if it had fallen into place, into sync.

Working swiftly, ignoring his patient's angry shouts of pain and bitten-off half curses, Dan fashioned a make-shift splint. All he needed was to have it hold until they could get Murphy to the clinic.

Rising, he looked toward Jake. "We need to take him back to the clinic."

Jake sighed dramatically. "I figured as much. Man never did nothing simple," he complained, shaking his head as he looked down at his friend.

Murphy took offense. "Nobody's telling you to hang around," he growled.

Jake hooted. "Then who'd pull your bacon out of the fire?"

The question obviously hit a sore spot. "Don't need it pulled out by nobody," Murphy declared angrily. "I can pull out my own bacon."

"Why don't you two settle all that later?" Tina suggested, raising her voice and cutting in like a mother refereeing two squabbling children. "Right now Doc needs you to concentrate on getting over to the clinic. Understood?" she asked sternly.

"Understood," Jake mumbled.

"Yeah," Murphy acknowledged even more quietly.

Dan merely grinned, amused. Tina was certainly something. Dynamite in a diminutive container. He could feel the smile spreading inside of him.

Getting his mind back on what needed doing, he indicated for Jake to get on Murphy's other side. After draping one of his arms on each of their shoulders, between the two of them, they lifted the injured man into an upright position.

Murphy yelled in protest throughout the entire process.

"Sorry, this is going to keep on hurting until I can get a cast on that leg and some painkillers into you," Dan predicted.

Wincing as Murphy screamed again, Jake had a proposition for the doctor. "How about you just hit him in the head with a hammer?"

"It's a thought," Dan muttered, doing his best to block out the man's cries.

"How about we hit *you* with a hammer?" Murphy cried irritably to his friend.

Maneuvering was difficult and slow, even with Tina trying to lead the way and kick aside the worst mounds. "Shut up, old man, or the next time I ain't calling nobody when I hear you screaming in pain," Jake threatened.

As they made progress toward the front door, Dan had to ask, "Why do you *keep* all this stuff?"

Jake inclined his head, peering at him from around his friend's torso. "I thought you said it was a disease."

"It is," he acknowledged. "Doesn't mean I understand it. You *really* need to clear out this place," he told his patient. "You're not going to be able to get around here otherwise. Especially not with your leg in a cast."

"I'll manage," Murphy sniffed indignantly. "And I'm gonna get this all cleared out. Been meaning to get around to it for a while now," he confessed, saying it as if it was gospel.

Apparently Jake knew better. "Ha!"

Murphy took the sound as a battle cry. "You wait and see, old man," he snapped at his friend. "You just wait and see. I'm gonna get to it."

"Yeah," Jake agreed, angling out of the front door with his burden. "When pigs fly."

"Before that," Murphy growled. And then he cried out sharply in pain again as Dan and Jake tried to get him into the backseat of Dan's car.

Dan shook his head. This wasn't going to work and he knew it. "There's no way I can get him into that." And then he heard himself making a suggestion that would have never even occurred to him when he was back in New York. "We're going to need a truck so he can lie in the flatbed."

"I'll go get mine," Jake volunteered, hurrying off to where he'd parked his vehicle.

"That house is a health hazard. It really needs to be cleared out," Dan said to Tina as they waited for Jake to return.

"I said I've been meaning to," Murphy protested.

Tina said nothing. But Dan had a feeling from the expression on her face that she had definitely come up with a thought on the matter. He also had a feeling that now wasn't the time to ask.

At least, not in front of his patient. But, knowing Tina, this was going to be good.

The subtle ease with which the phrase had gone through his head suddenly struck him.

Knowing Tina.

He hadn't realized, until just now, that it was true. He *did* know her, knew the workings of her mind. And he found an extreme source of heartwarming comfort in that.

As well as something more. Something, Dan knew in his heart, had been missing from his life until just recently.

He smiled to himself and focused on his patient.

Chapter Fifteen

There were several patients already standing outside the clinic, waiting to see Dan when they arrived back.

Several patients and one man Tina didn't recognize. In his early thirties with a privileged air about him, the man definitely didn't belong here. As it was, he stood apart from the four patients, an expression of vague amusement on his dark, handsome face.

Unlocking the front door, she let them in. The next moment, her attention was diverted as concern and questions came from the other people entering the waiting room.

"What happened to him?"

"Not enough business, Doc?" Henry Albert chuckled. "Goin' out and drummin' it up yourself?"

"Anything I can do to help?"

The last question came from Miss Joan. She stood in the doorway, having come in a beat after them. One of her customers had reported that Dan was bringing an injured George Murphy into the clinic. Her desire to be on top of any and all news had her driving over just in time to see the procession from the truck into the clinic.

He had enough helping hands, Dan thought. But there *was* something that Miss Joan could do. "Yes, there is. Why don't you see if you can get someone to make Mr. Murphy's house inhabitable again."

"I can take care of my own damn place," Murphy grumbled.

Miss Joan ignored the man's protest. She and Murphy went way back. "Knew this would happen to you some day, George. You've just got too much junk in that place of yours."

As other voices in the waiting room joined in with questions and helpful comments of their own, George Murphy began to holler with pain.

"Let's get him into the first exam room," Dan said to Jake. Tina hurried ahead to open the door for them. "It's the bigger of the two."

"You got it, Doc," Jake answered, trying not to sound as if he was panting. "You could stand to lose some weight, George."

Because, in all likelihood, he would keep the patients waiting for a bit, Dan felt he had to say something to them. "Sorry, folks. You're going to have to wait a little longer. I've got to set Mr. Murphy's leg."

"We understand, Doc. Just help old George there," Edna O'Malley told him. At eighty, she was the oldest patient in the room and felt she was speaking for all of them.

"Want a hand?"

The deep-voice, rumbling offer came from the

stranger on the far side of the room. As he made it, he rose to his feet.

The vaguely familiar voice had Dan turning his head rather than just telling the person that he and Tina would handle it from here. It didn't even occur to Dan until later just how much he'd come to, consciously and unconsciously, rely on Tina.

That epiphany along with everything else, temporarily faded in the face of his surprise.

It couldn't be.

Even as he looked at the man, for one moment he thought he was just imagining him.

"Knox?" The man's surname came to his lips almost involuntarily.

By now, Dan was aware that he had a curious audience as everyone in the waiting room, including Tina, eyed the stranger and him, apparently waiting for some further clue to be tossed their way.

Dr. William Knox, neurosurgeon, grinned and spread his hands before him as if prepared to be examined more closely. "In the flesh."

Knox was possibly the last man on earth Dan would have expected to see in Forever. "What are you doing here?"

"I've come to see what *you're* doing here." Knox nodded at the less-than-jovial-looking man currently being held up between Dan and a tall, wiry man. "So, do you need a hand, Davenport?"

Except on those occasions when he'd taken trips to the hospital at Pine Ridge for supplies, Dan hadn't so much as seen, much less talked to, another doctor. The familiar face of his fellow resident and one-time drinking buddy felt like a godsend.

"Hell, yes," Dan answered. "Two hands if you can spare them."

Bill Knox held his up as if to demonstrate. "Got 'em right here at your disposal, Dan." He moved in to take the older man's place, easing Jake out of the way. "Here, I'll take over," Knox told him, not expecting any sort of opposition.

Jake stepped back, looking a little miffed but saying nothing as he obligingly nodded his head.

Stunned by this sudden turn of events, and possibly a little worried, Tina called after Dan. "What do you want me to do?"

"Just stay with the patients," Dan answered without bothering to turn around or look over his shoulder. It was obvious that the stranger and Murphy had his full attention.

There was an uneasy feeling in the pit of Tina's stomach that she couldn't quite understand. She did her best to ignore it. There was nothing to worry about. Everything was going to be fine.

"Right," Tina murmured, more to herself than to Dan.

The second the door to exam room one closed, the waiting room suddenly swelled with the sound of raised voices. Questions went flying back and forth, aided and abetted by half-formed speculations.

When one of the people in the room put the question to Tina, asking who the man with Dan was, it was Miss Joan who stepped in to answer.

"Don't you have eyes, Fred? He's obviously a doctor who Doc knew back in New York City. A friend would be my guess since he came all the way out to see how Doc was doing," Miss Joan added.

"Think maybe he'll stay?" Mrs. O'Malley asked hopefully. "Two doctors are always better than one." The woman's face was positively cherubic as she smiled. "And he's cute."

"Not as good-looking as Doc," Miss Joan said loyally. "I've gotta be getting back. The girls don't like me leaving them for long." The last sentence was addressed to Tina.

Tina smiled. The woman had a very gruff way of mothering her, but she'd gotten used to it over the months and really did appreciate the woman's efforts.

"How long a wait, you think?" Fred Anderson pressed Tina as she returned to her desk.

On her way out, Miss Joan stopped to look over her shoulder at the man.

"Doc'll be done when he's finished," she informed Fred matter-of-factly, sparing Tina the trouble. "Why? You've got somewhere else to be?" It was clear by her tone that she knew he didn't.

The retired railroad engineer raised his wide shoulders in a hapless shrug. Very few people ever foolishly went toe-to-toe with Miss Joan. "Just asking," he mumbled timidly.

"And I'm just answering, Fred. No harm intended," Miss Joan told him. She glanced one last time at Tina. "See you later, honey. If you need to hang around longer," she said as an afterthought occurred to her, "don't worry about Bobby. Lupe's bringing him to the diner when she starts her shift. The little guy won't lack having eyes watching him," she promised.

It wasn't that she wasn't grateful, she was. But at this point, Tina couldn't help thinking, the women who worked in the diner saw her son more than she did. She would have to cut back on the accounts she handled out of the house, she decided. Working at the medical clinic took up a great deal of her time and whatever time she had left—that wasn't spent with Dan—needed to be devoted to Bobby or he would grow up thinking he had half a dozen "Mommies" and she would just be part of the group.

He slept less these days and wanted to play more. She really didn't want to miss out on this part of his life.

But she also didn't want to miss being with Dan, she thought ruefully.

To his credit, Dan spent a lot of time with her *and* Bobby. Still, it would be a lot easier if they were actually a *real* family unit, she mused. But for that to happen, a couple of steps in between were needed.

You can't rush this. All good things take time to come around. You know that.

She did know that. She just wished she could bridle her impatience a little better. Waiting was not one of her fortes.

The next moment, Fred Anderson approached her with another question obviously on his mind and she put her own thoughts and life on hold to give her job her full attention. After all, Dan depended on her to keep things running smoothly, she reminded herself.

The idea of Dan depending on her pleased her a great deal.

IT HAD BEEN A ROUGH AFTERNOON, following on the heels of a rougher morning. But it would have been a completely overwhelming zoo, Dan readily acknowledged, if he hadn't had Bill Knox pitching in and working right beside him. As it was, he'd not only had to deal with George Murphy's broken leg, but another two emergencies, back-to-back, in the afternoon. Emergencies that had to be worked into what was a full complement of patients for both the morning and the afternoon.

But even with the rancher whose horse had managed to throw him and then stomp on his hand, and another who'd gotten his hand impaled on the prong of a pitchfork, things had gone far more smoothly than they had since he'd first arrived in Forever.

That afternoon, the parade of patients had been nonstop for close to four hours straight. And then, finally, the last patient had been seen and treated.

From the sound of it, the reception area was devoid of anyone waiting to see him. Relieved, exhausted but extremely satisfied, Dan collapsed in a chair. He gestured toward the other one in his office, indicating that Knox follow suit.

The latter did, sliding practically bonelessly into the seat. Knox looked even more exhausted than he felt, Dan thought.

"Damn, this is like our E.R. days," Knox complained.

His eyes narrowed as he looked toward his friend. "Is it always this crazy here?"

"No," Dan answered, tongue in cheek. "This whole day was just for your benefit."

"Thanks," Bill said sarcastically. The next moment, he sat up and leaned into his friend. "So, tell me, what's the deal with Miss Hottie in the waiting room?"

The smile on Dan's lips retreated a little. He found that he took offense at the glib term that Knox was applying to Tina. "She's not a hottie—"

Knox laughed shortly. "Then you've gone blind, my friend. From where I'm sitting—"

Dan didn't want Knox to finish his thought. "She's a nice girl."

That only seemed to urge Knox on. "The best kind of hottie," he assured him. "She's yours exclusively, until you don't want her anymore," Knox concluded with a knowing air that Dan found extremely abrasive.

Had he been that shallow, that callous-sounding when he was back in New York? Dan couldn't help suddenly wondering. He hardly related to the man he'd been anymore. In an effort to move to better ground, Dan tried to guide the conversation in another direction. "So, you still haven't told me. What are you really doing out here? We don't have any five-star hotels."

"Listen to you," Knox hooted. "'We.' What 'we'? You're not part of this place. And I told you," Knox reminded him. "I came to see you. To find out if you've gotten tired of slumming and playing the dedicated doctor yet."

Dan tried not to lose his temper, reminding himself

that he and Knox had history and did go way back. "I'm not playing—"

"Sure you are," Knox insisted with a mocking laugh. "Don't get up on your righteous soapbox with me. This is Knox you're talking to. I've seen your dark soul. This is just something you felt you had to do, I get that. But if you recall, you had the good sense to give yourself a time limit to being a martyr. Nine months or until another doctor could be found, whichever came first, remember?" he prodded. "Well, I'm here to tell you that you don't have to wait any longer to go back home."

Dan felt himself growing rigid. "There's a doctor coming out?" he asked in a low, deliberately unemotional voice, not trusting himself to speak any louder.

"No, but these people waited all this time for one, they can wait a little longer," Knox argued. "You've got a life to get back to, Danny-boy. A damn special career waiting for you. It's not going to wait forever, you know. That medical firm will bring someone else in if you take too long getting back."

With a sigh, he drew his chair in closer to Dan, as if the closer proximity would somehow add weight to his words.

"You can't just throw it all away because some jerk plowed into the cab you and Warren were in and killed Warren. That wasn't your fault," he argued. "And even if it was, that's no reason to throw everything you worked for all those years away just like that. You're not thinking with your head," Knox said, tapping his forehead for emphasis.

Dan jerked his head back, annoyed. "You don't understand—"

"I understand," Knox interrupted. "You feel guilty. So, give them some money." By his tone, it was obviously the perfect solution to the other doctor. "This place looks like it could sure use some money dropped on it. What was it you called it when Warren said he was coming out here?" Knox tried to remember. Then did. "Dogpatch? Well, from what I see, it really is Dogpatch. And *you* don't belong here. You knew it three months ago, before you left on this penance mission. Nothing's changed."

Knox sighed, seeing that he was making no headway. "Look, Dan, if it makes you feel less guilty, I'll see if I can talk Lieberwitz into coming here and taking your place. You remember Stan Lieberwitz, right?"

Knox couldn't be serious. Dan vividly remembered Stan Lieberwitz. He'd spent countless nights tutoring the man, trying to give him a workable system to remember in order to pass his tests.

"He barely graduated at the bottom of our class. There was *no one* under him."

"Hey, they still call him 'doctor,' don't they?" he reminded Dan. "And that's all these people need, a doctor. Where does it say it's gotta be a doctor who's throwing away a damn good future, who graduated, at the last minute, with honors for God sakes?" He rose to emphasize his point. "Tell me you'll at least consider it, Danny-boy. Please. Now, where do you go in this two-bit town for a good time?"

To Tina. I go to Tina, Dan caught himself thinking.

But he knew he couldn't make his friend understand. Because three months ago, he had been just like Knox and he hadn't understood Warren when Warren had tried to get him to see his point of view. That there were things that went beyond prestige and an enviable position in the hierarchy.

Oh, he'd humored Warren, but he hadn't understood. Not until he'd come here and worked among real, decent people who needed him and who were there for one another without question.

He'd found something far more precious here than the envy of his peers. He'd found a purpose.

"You can go get a bite to eat at the diner," Dan told him, knowing that wasn't what Knox meant.

"I wasn't thinking of eating," Knox answered. And then his eyes widened as, apparently, a horrible thought occurred to him. "Oh, God, don't tell me you've gone dry." He didn't wait for an answer but went with his assumption. "This is worse than I thought. I'm going to have to lead an intervention down here for you." It was hard to tell if Knox was serious. The man had a tendency to get carried away once in a while.

"I'm not the one who needs an intervention," Dan replied quietly.

"You are from where I'm standing," Knox assured him with a shake of his head.

He didn't want to argue and he didn't want to drive a wedge between them. "C'mon, let's get something into you and we'll talk about this later. Right now, you can just catch me up on what everyone is doing."

"That's easy. Everyone's worried about you," Knox said glibly, walking out with Dan.

But Dan hardly heard him. He was looking around the waiting room. It was empty. *Completely* empty. He knew that there were no more patients, but Tina always waited for him and they had dinner together. She hadn't said anything about leaving early.

"Tina?" His voice echoing back was his only answer. Dan called her name again, louder this time as he walked to the rear of the clinic. He thought perhaps he'd missed her on his way to the entrance.

He hadn't. She wasn't there, either.

Doubling back, Dan stopped at her desk. Opening the right drawer where she always deposited her purse, he saw that it was missing. That only meant one thing. She'd left for the night.

A cold fear suddenly materialized, taking hold of his gut and twisting it.

"What's wrong?" Knox asked, seeing the look on his face. "Was the hottie supposed to stay and wait for you? Did I interrupt something?" he asked with an unmistakable leer.

He didn't have time to humor his friend anymore. "Shut up, Knox," Dan snapped as he stormed toward the door.

It hit Knox like a ton of bricks. "You care about her, don't you?" he asked in amazement. "You actually care. Who'd have thought it?" A laugh accompanied the enlightenment. "Hey, I didn't mean to spoil anything for you with the hottie."

He'd had enough. Dan whirled around, grabbed his

precariously close-to-being-an-ex-friend by the shirt and growled, "Stop talking about her if you know what's good for you."

Knox spread his hands out in the universal sign of surrender, wanting to placate him. "Hey, I'm sorry. I didn't mean anything by it—"

Releasing him, Dan hurried out the door without another word.

"Okay," Knox called after him. "We'll talk later."

Dan blocked out the annoying noise, focusing only on the urgent need for damage control.

Now.

Chapter Sixteen

Tina's heart felt like lead in her chest as she drove away from the clinic.

How could she have been so stupid? So naively gullible? Hadn't she had enough lessons? What did it *take* for her to finally learn? Even lower forms of animal life eventually caught on to behavioral patterns. Was she really that dense?

Or just that stubbornly hopeful?

Using the back of her wrist, Tina angrily swiped away the trail of tears that slid down her face no matter how much she willed herself not to cry. It wasn't worth it.

He wasn't worth it.

Okay, so he'd never come right out and said he loved her—and now she knew the reason why—but he'd acted as if he did. Acted as if he really cared about her.

What d'you expect? For him to kick you out of bed? Of course he acted like he loved you. How else was he going to get you to make love with him?

No, not make love, she corrected angrily. Have sex. That's what he was doing while she was making love. He was having sex. Cold, unadorned, unadulterated sex, nothing more. Very good sex. Okay, exquisite sex. But bottom line, it was sex and had absolutely nothing to do with love.

She was an idiot to have believed it was anything else.

Who knew how long she would have gone on in her deluded ignorance if she hadn't overheard Dan and that other doctor talking? The door to Dan's office had been partially ajar and Knox's voice had carried out to the waiting room. Before she knew it, she'd caught herself eavesdropping.

And then she'd felt her stomach lurch, tightening so hard she thought that she was going to throw up. That was when she'd quickly taken her purse and left. Or as quickly as she could on legs that had gone numb—along with the rest of her.

Idiot! she upbraided herself, the tears streaming again.

Well, that was it. She was through with men altogether. No one was getting near her heart ever again. Except for Bobby. But that didn't count because he was her son.

Oh, God, this hurt so badly she didn't think she could stand it.

Taking a breath to steady herself, Tina forced her mind to focus and look through the windshield. She hadn't realized until this moment that she'd unconsciously driven to the diner. Habit.

Well, she might as well go collect Bobby and go home. She fervently wished that she didn't have to face Miss Joan but there was no getting around it.

Flipping open the mirror hidden inside the driver's side sun visor, Tina did what she could to repair her face and hide the very obvious signs of her distress. With any luck, Miss Joan was busy and she could just scoop Bobby up from one of the waitresses who watched over the boy.

Bracing herself, Tina pasted a smile on her face and walked into the diner.

When the door opened, Miss Joan looked over in her direction, saw Tina and smiled. "Hi, Baby Girl." And then, as she *really* looked at Tina, the smile faded. "Take over, Julie," she said sharply to the waitress closest to the counter.

Making her way around it, her eyes never leaving her goal, she was beside Tina in an instant. Miss Joan draped her arm around Tina and steered her toward the back of the diner and her tiny office. Only when she was inside the room and had closed the door behind them did she finally speak.

"What's wrong?" she asked.

Tina deliberately avoided the woman's eyes. "Nothing's wrong. I'm just tired, Miss Joan."

Circling until she stood in front of the young woman, Miss Joan lifted her chin with the crook of her finger and forced Tina to look at her.

"Don't you lie to me, Baby Girl," Miss Joan said firmly. "I can spot a lie a mile away. Now what's wrong?" she repeated.

Knowing it was futile to resist or stall, Tina told her. Actually, it was more like she completely broke down and poured out her heart. She told the woman everything she'd heard and everything she felt in the wake of that information.

Miss Joan listened in silence, nodding once or twice and making no excuses for Dan. Now wasn't the time, even though she had a feeling that what Tina'd heard was not all there was to the story. The fact was that she would have been willing to bet her soul on it, but Tina, Miss Joan knew, was too hurt to listen. The young woman needed to give herself a little time to process and to think it over.

There was a piece that was missing. A piece that, once it came to light, would make Tina feel much better. Miss Joan was sure of it.

"Go on home, Baby Girl," Miss Joan urged softly. "I'll keep Bobby here. One of the girls'll bring him over later." She squeezed Tina's hand, mutely comforting her. "Go out the back way," she instructed. "You don't want to walk by everyone out front right now," she assumed wisely.

Tina tried to smile her thanks, but her mouth just refused to curve. Pain weighed her down. "Thank you," she whispered.

Miss Joan smiled, patting her shoulder. "It's why I'm here," she answered simply.

Walking back out to the front of the diner after Tina had left, Miss Joan judged that it would only be a matter of time.

And she was right.

Actually, she thought, Dan had gotten here a lot sooner than she'd figured he would. That had to count for something.

Miss Joan made herself both visible and accessible, but offered him no greeting as she cleaned the surface of a counter that needed no cleaning.

DAN'S HEART WAS POUNDING as he burst in through the diner's front door. Tina's car wasn't out front, but he hoped she was here. He knew that she regarded Miss Joan as a second mother, and Miss Joan could always be found here. It was only natural that this was where he'd find Tina.

Except that he didn't.

Not unless she was in the back office, Dan suddenly thought, remembering that Tina did do Miss Joan's accounts. A small ray of hope lit up the darkness inside of him.

"Miss Joan—" he began as he approached the counter.

Miss Joan glanced up as if this was the first she was aware of his presence. But instead of offering a greeting, she merely told him, "She doesn't want to see you."

That froze him in his tracks. He glanced around the diner, as if he'd somehow missed seeing Tina when he'd scanned the area. "Then she's here?"

Miss Joan shook her head. "Not anymore."

What did that mean? Before he could ask, Dan suddenly heard Bobby squeal gleefully. Turning, he saw the boy standing up in a small, makeshift playpen. The enclosure, with mesh running along its sides, was tucked over in the corner.

"She wouldn't have left without Bobby," he said accusingly.

"Nobody said anything about leaving," Miss Joan informed him. "What I said was that she's not here."

"Then where is she?" Dan had demanded.

"You're a bright boy. You figure it out," Miss Joan returned.

A soul-draining sigh escaped Dan's lips as he turned to go out again. Right now, his option was to drive around the town and hope he'd spot her.

But even as he made up his mind on his next course of action, he took a moment to walk over to Bobby's playpen and pause for a second.

Seeing him, Bobby began to jump up and down excitedly in anticipation of getting a playmate for however short a period of time.

Dan ruffled the boy's soft, still downy hair. "Can't stop and play with you right now, kid," he told the little boy. "But I'm coming back and I'll make it up to you. We'll play later. After I find your mom."

As he began to walk out the door, Miss Joan called out to him. "Go easy on her. She's very vulnerable right now."

"Makes two of us, Miss Joan," he said under his breath as he left.

He went to Tina's sister's house first and only met disappointment there, not to mention that he also had to field several questions about why he was looking for Tina in the first place since she was supposedly working for him.

"Her picking up and disappearing days are behind her." Olivia told him what she had come to firmly believe. The new mother had come to the front door, her tiny daughter comfortably nestled and asleep against her shoulder.

He fervently hoped so, Dan thought as he apologized to Olivia for disturbing her.

Retreating, he got back behind the wheel of his car and thought for a moment. Could Tina have just gone home? Was it as simple as that? He hadn't thought it could be that easy.

He'd assumed she would be seeking solace from her friends, not going where she could be alone. He learned something about Tina every day and desperately wanted the lessons to continue. Indefinitely.

Arriving at Miss Joan's small, two-story house he got out of the car and walked up to the front door—where he stood for several beats, getting up the courage to confront Tina. Trying not to think that he might not be able to convince her that he didn't share Knox's opinion of things. He wasn't going to get anywhere standing out here like some coward, afraid to take hold of his own life.

Dan rang the doorbell and then, impatient, knocked half a second after that.

On the other side of the door, Tina came hurrying over to answer it, thinking that maybe Miss Joan had changed her mind and decided to send Lupe over with Bobby after all.

Swinging the door open, she started talking to Lupe before she realized that it wasn't the waitress standing on the doorstep with her son.

It was Dan.

Hot anger raced through Tina, smothering the quick,

almost involuntary shaft of happiness that had shot through her when she saw him there.

That was just a knee-jerk reaction, nothing more, she told herself. The anger, though, was well deserved. Furious, Tina tried to swing the door shut again, but he was too quick for her, putting his foot in the way to keep the door from meeting the jamb.

He braced the door with his hand, keeping it in place. "Please, Tina, let me in."

"Not anymore," she snapped, stubbornly trying to push the door closed. It was no contest. He was too strong for her. "I'm going to purge you out of my life," she shouted. "Go back to New York with your friend where you belong!"

Dan pushed harder and succeeded in getting her to back up and out of the way. Walking in, he informed her, "I don't belong in New York."

"Oh, no?" Her eyes narrowed into angry slits. How stupid did he think she was? "That's where your friend thinks you belong. And from what he said, that's what you think, too."

He wasn't about to lie to her. "I did," he acknowledged, then quickly added, "but I don't anymore."

"Oh?" The edge in her voice mocked him. "And what changed your mind?" she asked, her voice growing harder. She didn't believe him for a minute.

Dan looked into her eyes and answered quietly. "You."

He was lying to her. Staring right into her eyes and lying. Incensed, she hit him across the face before she even knew she was going to do it.

Tina squared her shoulders, glaring angrily at him. "Just how stupid do you think I am?"

He rubbed his cheek. For a small thing, she had quite a wallop. "Not stupid at all."

"Then why are you insulting me like that?" she demanded.

He didn't understand why she'd think that. "I'm not insulting you at all."

"What would you call it, then?" she asked. "What would you call thinking that I would believe a lie like that after what I heard in your office today?"

She had to be reasonable. She *was* reasonable. He had to believe that. Because he had nothing else to hang on to and winning her back was now the most important thing in his life.

The *only* thing in his life that mattered.

"I'm not sure what you heard or how much of it you heard," he began, "but if you listened, you had to have heard that I told Knox I didn't agree with him. That I told him to shut up."

Each step he took toward her, she took a step back. Her hands were on her hips as she looked at him defiantly. "Then you don't think I'm a 'hottie'?" she asked in an accusing voice.

"Of course I think you are. I mean no—" He shut his mouth, realizing that he was tripping over his tongue. Dan tried again. "You are extremely hot, Tina. But not in the cheap sort of sense that Knox was making it sound."

"An expensive 'hottie,'" Tina said mockingly. "Is that supposed to be better?"

He tried one more time, knowing he had a great deal to atone for. Not just with Tina, but for his cavalier past, as well. He could have been doing a lot of good so much sooner.

"You are a gorgeous woman, Tina, and in that sense you could be described with that ridiculous term. But all that kind of talk belongs to another world. A world I was part of, yes," he allowed, "but a world I don't belong in anymore."

She could feel herself wavering and tried desperately to stand firm. "Okay, let's just say I believe you—which I don't," she quickly and sharply qualified, "just where is it that you think you do belong?"

There wasn't a moment's hesitation. He knew. "Here. With you."

She wasn't falling for this, she wasn't. "Until they send another doctor."

"No," he contradicted, making her a promise whether she knew it or not, "until I die."

She tore her eyes away from his. He wasn't going to get to her. She'd promised herself that less than an hour ago, hadn't she? "Which might be very soon if you don't stop lying to me."

"I'm not lying, Tina," he told her as sincerely as he could. He didn't know what else to do. "Yes, I came here thinking it was only for a few months. I gave myself nine at the most. A nine-month sentence," he acknowledged since that was the way he'd viewed it. "But I felt I owed it to Warren to come."

She picked up on the fact that he was using past tense. "And now?" she asked.

"And now I owe it to me to stay," he told her simply. "I never realized what making a difference felt like or really meant," he confessed. "To the people who come into the clinic. To see me because they think I can help them." His voice took on depth and feeling as he continued. "I *like* making a difference. I like that people *think* I make a difference. None of that factored into my life before," he admitted.

Tina blew out a breath, afraid to believe him. Wanting to believe him more than she wanted to breathe. She felt so torn.

"So you're staying because you want to be Albert Schweitzer." The mocking tone was not quite harsh.

That was one way to put it, he supposed. Dan smiled for the first time since he'd banged on her door. "I'm staying because I want to be Albert Schweitzer—and I'm staying because this is where you are."

Her eyes narrowed. He would cajole her now, she thought. "And what do I have to do with it?"

He took a chance. Standing in front of her, he threaded his arms around her waist and took a chance that she wouldn't push him away. That she'd hear him out. All she had to do was listen to one word. It said it all.

"Everything," he answered softly.

She braced her hands on top of his arms as if to push him away.

Except that she didn't.

She left her hands there as she looked up into his eyes, telling herself that she'd know if he was lying. That she'd see a spark of hesitation there. Except that she didn't.

What she saw in his eyes, she realized, was herself. *She* was what was reflected back at her.

"Go on," she told him quietly.

Dan pressed his lips together, choosing his words carefully. Knowing that he had just one shot at this and he couldn't mess it up.

"I love you." There it was, simple and unadorned. Dan shook his head and said disparagingly, "They used to say I could sweet-talk the feathers off a dove, but I seem to have lost the knack."

He'd just told her he loved her, without any fanfare. He'd snared her heart with those three words, there was no point in pretending to herself that he hadn't.

"You're doing fine," she murmured.

He felt as if he was standing on a tightrope, using only one leg to balance himself. Feeling very, very uncertain. "Then you believe me?"

"Are you lying?" she asked quietly.

"No," he answered with feeling.

She struggled to keep her smile under wraps. If she let it burst through, it would ruin a good moment. He deserved to be on pins and needles for a couple more seconds at the very least. "Then I believe you. Anything else?"

"Yes." The relief was enormous. He almost couldn't process its effect. "Whether you like it or not, I plan to go on loving you for the rest of my life."

"Why?" She needed an answer to that before she felt secure. Didn't matter what kind or how extensive, so long as he had a reason. Because then she knew that Dan really would stay.

"Because you make me happy. Because you make me realize I wasn't whole before and I am now. Because I want us to be a family, you, Bobby and me. Because—"

Laughing now, she put her finger to his lips, stopping the flow. "Shhh. Stop talking," she coaxed, rising up on her toes to kiss him.

Taking hold of her shoulders, he stopped her at the last second. She looked at him quizzically. "Do you love me?"

Her eyes, so solemn, so hurt only minutes ago, were full of mischief as Tina regarded him. "What do you think?"

He was about to say "yes," but he didn't get the chance. Her lips had sealed his and he suddenly had far more important things to do than talk.

* * * * *

Harlequin®

COMING NEXT MONTH

Available April 12, 2011

#1349 MY FAVORITE COWBOY
American Romance's Men of the West
Shelley Galloway

#1350 ONE WILD COWBOY
Texas Legacies: The McCabes
Cathy Gillen Thacker

#1351 A CONVENIENT PROPOSAL
Creature Comforts
Lynnette Kent

#1352 RODEO DADDY
Rodeo Rebels
Marin Thomas

REQUEST YOUR FREE BOOKS!
2 FREE NOVELS PLUS 2 FREE GIFTS!

 Harlequin®

 American ★ Romance®

LOVE, HOME & HAPPINESS

YES! Please send me 2 FREE Harlequin American Romance® novels and my 2 FREE gifts (gifts are worth about $10). After receiving them, if I don't wish to receive any more books, I can return the shipping statement marked "cancel." If I don't cancel, I will receive 4 brand-new novels every month and be billed just $4.24 per book in the U.S. or $4.99 per book in Canada. That's a saving of at least 15% off the cover price! It's quite a bargain! Shipping and handling is just 50¢ per book in the U.S. and 75¢ per book in Canada.* I understand that accepting the 2 free books and gifts places me under no obligation to buy anything. I can always return a shipment and cancel at any time. Even if I never buy another book, the two free books and gifts are mine to keep forever.

154/354 HDN FDKS

Name _____ (PLEASE PRINT) _____

Address _____ Apt. # _____

City _____ State/Prov. _____ Zip/Postal Code _____

Signature (if under 18, a parent or guardian must sign)

Mail to the **Reader Service:**
IN U.S.A.: P.O. Box 1867, Buffalo, NY 14240-1867
IN CANADA: P.O. Box 609, Fort Erie, Ontario L2A 5X3

Not valid for current subscribers to Harlequin American Romance books.

Want to try two free books from another line?
Call 1-800-873-8635 or visit www.ReaderService.com.

* Terms and prices subject to change without notice. Prices do not include applicable taxes. Sales tax applicable in N.Y. Canadian residents will be charged applicable taxes. Offer not valid in Quebec. This offer is limited to one order per household. All orders subject to credit approval. Credit or debit balances in a customer's account(s) may be offset by any other outstanding balance owed by or to the customer. Please allow 4 to 6 weeks for delivery. Offer available while quantities last.

Your Privacy—The Reader Service is committed to protecting your privacy. Our Privacy Policy is available online at www.ReaderService.com or upon request from the Reader Service.

We make a portion of our mailing list available to reputable third parties that offer products we believe may interest you. If you prefer that we not exchange your name with third parties, or if you wish to clarify or modify your communication preferences, please visit us at www.ReaderService.com/consumerschoice or write to us at Reader Service Preference Service, P.O. Box 9062, Buffalo, NY 14269. Include your complete name and address.

HARI I

Selene wanted nothing to do with the father of her son, Alex; but Aristedes had other plans...that included them.

Read on for an sneak peek from
THE SARANTOS SECRET BABY by Olivia Gates,
available April 2011, only from Harlequin Desire.

"You were right to turn my marriage offer down," Aristedes said.

And Selene found her voice at last, found the words that would not betray the blow he'd dealt her. "Thanks for letting me know. You didn't have to come all the way here, though. You could have just let it go. I left yesterday with the understanding that this case is closed."

Before the hot needles behind her eyes could dissolve into an unforgivable display of stupidity and weakness, she began to close the door.

The door stopped against an immovable object. His flat palm.

"I can't accept that." His voice was low, leashed.

What did her tormentor mean now? Was he ending one game only to start another?

She raised eyes as bruised as her self-respect to his, found nothing there but solemnity and determination.

Before she could voice her confusion, he elaborated. "I never let anything go unless I'm certain it's unworkable. I realize I made you an unworkable offer, and that's why I'm withdrawing it. I'm here to offer something else. A workability study."

She leaned against the door, thankful for its support and partial shield. "Your son and I are not a business venture you can test for feasibility."

His gaze grew deeper, made her feel as if he was trying to delve into her mind, take control of it. "It's actually the other way around. I'm the one who would be tested."

She shook her head. "Why bother? I know—and *you* know—you're not workable. Not with me."

His spectacular eyebrows lowered over eyes she felt were emitting silver hypnosis. "You're right again. Neither you nor I have any reason to believe that isn't the truth. The only truth. It might be best for both you and Alex to never hear from me again, to forget I exist. But then again, maybe not. I'm only asking for the chance for both of us to find out for certain. You believe I'm unworkable in any personal relationship. I've lived my life based on that belief about myself. I never really had reason to question it. But I have one now. In fact, I have two."

Find out what happens in
THE SARANTOS SECRET BABY by Olivia Gates,
available April 2011, only from Harlequin Desire.